Whose dark or troubled mind will you step into next? Detective or assassin, victim or accomplice? How can you tell reality from delusion when you're spinning in the whirl of a thriller, or trapped in the grip of an unsolvable mystery? When you can't trust your senses, or anyone you meet; that's when you know you're in the hands of the undisputed masters of crime fiction.

Writers of the greatest thrillers and mysteries on earth, who inspired those that followed. Their books are found on shelves all across their home countries – from Asia to Europe, and everywhere in between. Timeless tales that have been devoured, adored and handed down through the decades. Iconic books that have inspired films, and demand to be read and read again. And now we've introduced Pushkin Vertigo Originals – the greatest contemporary crime writing from across the globe, by some of today's best authors.

So step inside a dizzying world of criminal masterminds with **Pushkin Vertigo**. The only trouble you might have is leaving them behind.

FRÉDÉRIC DARD

PUSHKIN VERTIGO

BIRD IN A CAGE

TRANSLATED FROM THE FRENCH BY DAVID BELLOS

Pushkin Vertigo
71–75 Shelton Street
London, WC2H 9JQ

Original text © 1961 Fleuve Editions,
département d'Univers Poche, Paris

First published in French as *Le Monte-Charge* in 1961

Translation © David Bellos, 2016

First published by Pushkin Vertigo in 2016

1 3 5 7 9 8 6 4 2

ISBN 978 1 782271 99 4

Text designed and typeset by Tetragon, London
Printed and bound by CPI Group (UK) Ltd, Croydon CR0 4YY

www.pushkinpress.com

To Philippe Poire,
my faithful reader,
from his faithful author

F.D.

1

The Encounter

How old does a man have to be not to feel like an orphan when he loses his mother?

When I returned after being away for six years to the small flat where Mother died, it felt like the slipknot on a rope round my chest was being tightened without pity.

I sat down in the old armchair next to the window where she always did the darning and looked around at the silence, the smell and all the old things that had lain waiting for me. The silence and the smells had greater reality for me than the damp-streaked wallpaper.

My mother died four years ago and I learned of her death only when I got the funeral notice. I'd thought about her a lot since then but I hadn't wept for her enormously. Now, as I crossed the threshold of our flat, I suddenly grasped that she had died. It hit me head-on.

Outside, it was Christmas.

What brought it home to me was coming back to Paris and to the crowded boulevards of its poorer districts lined with brightly lit shop window displays, and with illuminated trees at street corners.

Christmas!

I was a fool to come home on a day like that.

There was a smell that I didn't recognize in her bedroom—the smell of her dying. The bed had been entirely stripped and the mattress rolled up in an old sheet. The people who took care of her had forgotten to take away the glass for the holy water and the sprig of blessed palm.

These sorry items were on the marble dresser next to a black wooden crucifix. There was no water left in the glass and the leaves on the sprig had gone yellow. When I picked it up, they fell on the bedroom carpet like golden flakes.

There was a photograph of me on the wall in the ornate old frame that had been used to display my father's medals. The photo was about ten years old but it wasn't very flattering. I looked like a sickly and repressed young man, with hollow cheeks, a sidelong glance and the kind of vague pouting expression that could only belong to someone very bad or very miserable.

Only a mother's eyes could forgive a snap like that for being such a disappointment, and even find beauty in it.

I thought I was better looking now. The years had filled me out, and I had acquired a direct look and relaxed features.

I still had to say hello to my own room.

It was unchanged. My bed was made. The books I used to like were stacked on the mantelpiece, and next to the wardrobe key the little manikin I'd carved from a piece of hazel wood just for fun was still there.

I flopped onto the bed on my back. The bedspread had its familiar coarse feel and its good old smell of colourfast linen. I closed my eyes and said aloud, the way I used to in the morning to ask for my breakfast, "Hey there, Ma!"

Some people pray in a different way, with prepared sentences. But that simple call said in an everyday way was the best I could do. For a very short moment I hoped that by concentrating with all my heart and soul the past might answer me back. I think I would have given the rest of my life without a second thought to see my mother for just a second, standing behind the door. Yes, I'd give anything just to hear her asking in that voice of hers which was always slightly anxious when she talked to me, "Are you awake, my dear?"

I was awake.

And a whole life would pass by before I could go back to sleep.

My spoken words went on expanding and vibrating and filling the silence of the flat long enough to allow me to feel all the sorrow it held.

It wasn't possible to spend the evening in here. I needed noise, light and drink. I needed life!

In the wardrobe I found my imitation camelhair coat with the mothballs Ma had naturally provided. It used to be a "generous" fit but now it was tight on my shoulders.

As I put it on I looked at my other clothes hanging inside their dust covers. These old outfits that no longer suited me seemed so crass! They spoke of my past more eloquently than my own memories.

They alone could say exactly what I had been.

I went out. Or rather, I fled.

The stair lady was muttering curses as she swept. Still the same old woman. When I was a lad she already had that worn-out look of someone who'd come to the end of the line. I used to think of her as exceedingly old—almost older than she looked now. She looked at me without recognizing my face. Her eyes had got worse; and I had changed.

Oily drizzle was falling in stops and starts and the gleaming roadway multiplied the streetlamps. The narrow streets of Levallois were full of happy people. They were knocking off work bearing Christmas supplies and thronging around open-air stalls where fishmongers shucked bucket-loads of oysters under wreaths of coloured lights.

The delis and cake shops were packed. A limping paper-hawker zigzagged from one pavement to the other calling out the news, but nobody gave a damn.

I walked on aimlessly, churning over the sorrow that gripped me in the gut. I stopped in front of the narrow window of a small book and stationery shop that also sold odds and ends. It was one of those local shops where you can get all kinds of stuff: prayer books in the season of first communions, fireworks around the 14th of July, exercise books at the start of the school year and Christmas decorations in December. Shops like that were all my youth, and I love them all the more as they decline and vanish.

That's why I felt so intensely the wish to go in and buy something, for the sole pleasure of the smell that brought back lost sensations.

Four or five women had squeezed into the narrow space. The saleslady looked like an aged widow. The look of someone in mourning forever! There was a smell of cocoa wafting from the room at the back.

I was glad there were people inside the shop. It meant I could linger, inspect its inexpensive treats and rediscover images of my childhood that I felt in special need of that day.

The place was like a fairy grotto piled high with glittering treasures. Christmas tree decorations were stacked on the shelves: glass birds, paper Father Christmases, baskets of fruit made of painted cotton and all those dainty balls as fragile as soap bubbles that help to make a tree into a fairy tale.

I was next to be served. There were people waiting behind me.

"What can I get you?"

I pointed to a silver cardboard birdcage sprinkled with glitter-dust. Inside it an exotic bird made of blue and yellow velvet stood on a golden perch.

"That one," I stammered.

"Will that be all?"

"Yes."

The saleslady put the cage in a little cardboard box and tied it up with a ribbon.

"Three twenty!"

When I went out I was feeling better. I couldn't grasp exactly why the purchase of a Christmas decoration I had no use for had suddenly put me back in touch with my past.

It was a mystery.

I went into a bar for an aperitif. The place was full of overexcited men talking about what they were going to do for the rest of the evening. Most of them had packets under their arms or in their pockets.

I was tempted to catch a bus to go and nose around the big department stores on the Grands Boulevards.

But when I thought about it I preferred to stay in my own neck of the woods. The crowd in Levallois was humbler but also noisier and warmer than in the centre of town. At every step I saw faces that "said something" to me but nobody recognized me.

At a crossing someone shouted out at the top of his voice "Albert!" I turned round like a flash. But it wasn't me that was meant, it was a tall spotty lad wearing a pastry cook's checkerboard jacket strenuously pedalling a delivery tricycle.

My old *quartier*! Its smell of wet soot and cooking oil! Its wobbly paving stones! Its dreary frontages! Its bars! Its stray dogs that the pound had given up trying to catch!

I walked for more than an hour under the greasy rain, taking my fill of a thousand tiny, heady, bittersweet emotions that took me back fifteen years. At that time I was in secondary school and Christmas had lost none of its magic.

Towards eight I went into a big restaurant in the centre. It was more like a traditional brasserie with mirrors, wooden mouldings, napkins in rings, huge leather bench seats with climbing plants behind them, a counter you could sit at and waiters in black trousers and white jackets.

There were check curtains on the windows and in summer the houseplants were put out on the pavement. The place had the feel of a "highly regarded" provincial establishment. And it certainly was well regarded. Throughout my childhood, whenever I turned up my nose at a meal my mother served, she would sigh, "So go and eat at Chiclet's!"

I did dream of being able to eat there one day. It seemed to me that only very wealthy and substantial people could afford such luxury. Every evening on my way home from school I stopped outside the restaurant and stared through its huge and misted windows at the opulent part of humanity holding court inside.

Outside mealtimes weighty gentlemen went there to play bridge. As the time to serve lunch or dinner drew nearer, the gaming tables would vanish one after the other like ships wrecked at sea. There was just one lifeboat left at the back of the room with waiters hovering impatiently around it until the truly indefatigable conceded the last rubber…

I went in for the first time in my life.

Although I'd been old enough and rich enough to patronize the restaurant before I went away, I had never dared go inside.

But that night I dared. And I did something more. I sauntered in. I dropped into Chiclet's like I was a regular.

During my long absence I had decided so often that I would go to Chiclet's when I got back, I had rehearsed so many times how I would stand and how I would move my arms that I was now performing an almost habitual act.

I had a momentary bout of dizziness because of the smell. I did not recognize it and could not have imagined it in advance. It wasn't like that of ordinary restaurants. Chiclet's smelled of absinthe and snails, and of old wood too.

At the back there was a very tall Christmas tree decked in fairy lights and tinsel that made the old-fashioned brasserie feel like a fairground.

The waiters had all pinned a tiny sprig of holly on their white jackets and the owners, M. and Mme Chiclet, stood at the bar serving free aperitifs to long-standing customers.

The couple had an elevated notion of the role of restaurateur. They were always dressed up to the nines, and gave the impression they were welcoming guests rather than serving customers.

She was a stout woman who, despite her dark dresses and chunky jewels, wasn't far removed from being just a blowsy cashier-at-a-big-café. He was a wan-faced man with thinning hair plastered down on the top of his skull who wore outdated suits. He must have been chair of a heap of trade bodies and waved his hand like a prelate to intervene in a debate or to give someone else the floor.

The dinner service had barely started and there weren't many customers yet. A splay-footed lad came up to take care of me. He helped to relieve me of my overcoat, hung it on a circular coat stand and, with a nod of his chin towards the restaurant, asked:

"Do you mind where?"

"Near the tree, if it's possible…"

I really would have liked to take my mother to Chiclet's. She had never been inside. She must have dreamed of it all her life as well!

I settled into the bench seat opposite the Christmas tree and ordered a fine repast. I suddenly felt all right. All right as when you're hungry and about to eat. All right as when you're tired and about to go to bed. The only real pleasure in the world is to satisfy a need.

What I was satisfying at that moment was not an appetite but a childhood dream.

I set about counting the number of lights on the tree. They

fascinated me. As I neared the end of that useless arithmetical exercise a small voice close by me gurgled:

"That's pretty."

I turned around and discovered a fairly ugly little girl of three or four sitting at the next table and also looking at the tree. The girl's head was a bit too large, her face was flat, her hair was reddish-brown and her nose like a radish. She resembled Shirley Temple as an infant prodigy. Yes, that was exactly right. Shirley Temple minus the good looks.

The child was with a woman, presumably her mother. She had seen me turn towards them and was smiling at me, as all mothers smile when you look at their child. I had a shock.

The woman looked like Anna. She had dark hair as Anna did, the same dark and almond-shaped eyes, the same dusky complexion and the same witty, sensual lips that scared me. She might have been twenty-seven, which is what Anna would have been. She was very pretty and smartly dressed. The little girl didn't have her eyes, or her hair, or her nose, but in spite of that she still managed to look like her mother.

"Eat up your fish, Lucienne!"

The child obediently forked a sliver of sole on her over-large plate. She steered it clumsily towards her mouth while looking all the time at the tree.

"It's big, isn't it?"

"Yes, darling."

"Did it grow here?"

I laughed. The woman looked at me again, and was visibly pleased by the way I had reacted. Our eyes crossed for a few seconds, then she lowered her gaze, as if I had upset her. I stole a glance at myself in the huge mirror opposite. I wasn't bad looking at all in a "battered by life" way. Wrinkles can be attractive in a thirty year old. I had a set of them in the corners of my eyes, plus a couple of very deep ones on my forehead.

There was something strange about a young woman and her daughter eating out in a restaurant on Christmas Eve. Seeing the two of them sent a pang to my heart. Their shared loneliness was more tragic than mine, which was, in the last analysis, pure and simple solitude.

The peace I'd felt since coming into the restaurant abruptly turned to gloom. All my life I'd suffered these sudden dips. I never knew how I'd feel from one minute to the next. I was always uneasy and permanently on the alert. I oozed anxiety and always had. It was painful, but I'd ended up getting used to it over the last six years.

I ate my oysters then my pheasant with straw chips, washing it down with a bottle of rosé. Now and again a remark by the girl gave me an excuse to look at her mother and each time I did so I felt the same shock at how much she looked like Anna. Our game lasted through the whole meal. I call it our game because the young woman passed the ball, so to speak. When I turned my head towards her, she turned towards me. And with perplexing regularity her face expressed in turn interest, then sadness, then modesty.

We finished our respective meals at almost the same time. The child's dawdling had made up for my late start. The woman ordered a coffee and the bill. I did the same.

The restaurant had filled up meanwhile. The waiters were racing around. You could hear orders being yelled in the kitchen like commands in the engine room of a ship. Conversations were getting louder. You could have been in a railway station. The clinking of cutlery and glassware and the popping sounds of corks being drawn made a lively melody, a hymn to earthy enjoyment that, because I'd now eaten, I found vaguely repugnant.

Waiting customers stood with their backs to the bar on the lookout for tables becoming available. Our bills were brought without delay; when they came back with the change, the waiters also brought our coats. Ravenous customers delighted to take our places were already gathering round our tables.

The woman buttoned up her daughter's velvet-collared woollen coat before putting on the astrakhan that the waiter was holding wide open for her, which made him look like a monstrous bat.

We came together again at the exit. I held the door open. She thanked me and her heart-rending gaze hit me point blank. She had eyes I couldn't describe but could have looked at for hours without stirring, without speaking, and maybe even without thinking.

They went out. The girl was whispering things that I couldn't hear and that her mother didn't seem to be listening to.

The rain had stopped and it was getting colder. A strange kind of cold in a winter that was too mild. There definitely would not be snow. Traffic was getting thinner. The cars that went past threw up wet mud. Some of the shops were beginning to close. I stood outside the restaurant like a post, without knowing what I was going to do. The woman's gaze was still inside me; it was taking time to evaporate.

She turned around twice as she walked down the street. She wasn't making an invitation, but she wasn't frightened either. It was just a quick look back, a completely instinctive gesture, I could feel it. She wanted to find out if I was going to follow them. She wasn't afraid of that, but she wasn't asking for it either.

I started off in the same direction. Let me be clear: I was not following them. I picked the same street simply because it was the way to my flat.

We covered a few hundred metres with a good distance between us. Then there was a crossroads and I lost sight of them. That was normal. I felt an unpleasant tightness in my chest, but I accepted a separation that was just as random as our meeting had been. Only I felt sad; sad like six years ago when I saw Anna dead. A disbelieving sadness. Something inside me would not accept the separation.

I continued on my way towards my flat.

As I passed by a cinema I saw them in the entrance gazing at the photos on display.

The mother was looking at the stills. As for the child, her eyes were fixed on the scrawny Christmas tree in the lobby.

It was a puny little pine from some suburban back garden. By way of decoration, photos of stars were hanging from its branches.

I knew that cinema well. It was the Majestic. I'd seen so many Westerns there, at the time I could have given you the title of any one of them just by listening to a few bars of the soundtrack.

I went into the lobby. The woman noticed me. It was as if she had been expecting me to crop up again. This time she scarcely looked at me but her face was suddenly drained of colour.

I realized that if I let her get to the ticket office before me I wouldn't have the courage to follow her. So I took the initiative. In the mirror behind the cashier I saw her come up behind me. I paid for my ticket. I moved away. She was there, holding her daughter by the hand.

"Two seats."

As at the restaurant I opened the door for them and as at the restaurant she looked "right through me". But this time she muttered a timid "thank you".

The film had already begun. It was a documentary about Ukraine: fields of ripening corn reaching as far as the eye could see.

An usherette dashed up to us, making signals with her pocket lamp. The woman gave her two tickets. The usherette probably didn't notice the little girl and so she thought we were together and seated us next to each other in a row quite near the front.

My heart was thumping wildly, like it had on the day when I went out with Anna for the first time. I sat bolt upright with my eyes on the screen, not seeing anything of what it showed and hearing nothing but the chaotic beating of my heart. I could feel the human warmth of the woman, and it overwhelmed me. The perfume of her overcoat shattered me.

Her daughter was asking questions aloud and the woman kept on leaning over towards her and whispering:

"Lucienne, be quiet. You are not supposed to talk!"

The child eventually stopped speaking. The documentary was coming to an end in any case and the house lights came back on.

I saw my dear old fleapit again. It hadn't been redecorated. It was still that nasty shade of dark red and it had kept its fluffy scarlet wall hangings, its squeaky seats and the greenery painted on cardboard at the foot of the screen.

An usherette went past, reciting the list of goodies in her tray in a bored and whining tone.

"Sweets!" the little girl cried.

It was a unique opportunity, an ideal if hardly original ploy. I was seated between the usherette and the woman. I could buy a packet of sweets and pass them to the child while mumbling an unanswerable, "May I, Madame?"

But instead of doing that I stayed stiff and inexpressive. I didn't even offer to act as a relay when the usherette held out the packet of sweets.

The interval ended. I was impatient for the lights to go down. Impatient to return to a state of reticent intimacy. I didn't even know what the film was called. That was the least of my worries.

Letters began parading across the screen but I had no wish to read them.

I fell back into the sense of ease and well-being that the restaurant had given me. It was primarily a sense of security, and being certain that I had a few minutes of real happiness ahead of me.

The little girl fell asleep. She started whining a little as she tried to find a comfortable position but couldn't. So her mother put her on her lap. The child's legs stuck into mine.

"Excuse me," the woman mumbled.

"You're welcome. I, er... You can let her stretch out."

But instead she put her hand around the girl's ankles to stop the child from kicking me.

That hand mesmerized me. I waited a bit as I tried to suppress the wish to grasp it gently and to hold it in mine. I needed that contact. I could imagine it. My own skin intuited what hers was like. I could have tried to play a trick, or to cheat a bit, by adopting a position on the armrest that would have allowed my hand to move quite naturally towards hers and brush her fingers in a way that would not cause her to take offence.

Yet again I didn't dare.

I turned towards her. She also looked at me. And it was so simple that I thought I would die of ecstasy, seeing how strong my will was.

I took her hand. She let go of the child's legs. Our fingers opened and then closed on each other as if we were praying together. It was strange, voluptuous and fierce.

I felt powerful, and, in a flash, six whole years were wiped away. I was with Anna. She was still alive and she loved me. She gave me her warmth, I gave her my strength.

Why did I want to lean towards this nameless woman and tell her:

"I love you."

Because I really did?

Many people imagine that love is a feeling that needs to be "set up", that it is the end of a process. I know that is not so, because I loved Anna and this woman from the very moment our eyes first met.

We stayed like that for a long time with fingers entwined, making love with our hands. Then the child kicked her legs and began to whimper in her sleep. Her mother withdrew her hand and it felt to me like a bereavement.

She whispered to the sleeping child:

"We're going home, my little Lucienne. You'll get back to sleep…"

She was speaking for me.

"If I may," I stammered.

I lifted the girl, settled her in my arms, and got up. She was heavy; she still smelt like a baby and sleep made her unappealing little face beautiful and touching.

I went up the aisle beside the woman. It felt as if I knew her intimately. Her gait had a rhythm that was familiar to me. Once we were in the lobby we looked at each other in the harsh light of the sickly neon. She looked a little tense and I was afraid it was in reaction to my presumptuousness.

On the other hand, had she not encouraged it?

"Do you have a car?"

"No, sir, I live nearby."

She cradled her arms.

"Thank you… She's not used to being up late."

"I'll walk you home."

She was expecting that, for sure, yet something in her eyes—whatever was it?—was unsteady. She stood still with her arms held out towards her child. Then she let them drop.

"Thank you."

And she set off without bothering about the two of us. I found it hard to keep up because the girl was getting heavier and heavier. It was the first time in my life that I had held a child in my arms and I would never have thought it could be so moving. I walked with great care: I was afraid of falling with such a precious cargo.

So on we went in single file to the end of the street. Then she turned right towards a newly built-up area that I didn't know because it had hardly existed when I had left.

These streets were less well lit. There weren't any more shops or shellfish stalls, and no more Christmas trees unless they were indoors, because there were hints of coloured lights gleaming in the windows.

Whitewashed buildings rose up in the shadows. That's where the woman was heading. She didn't say a word to me during the whole journey. You might have thought she'd forgotten about me and her daughter.

Two or three times the child struggled and I had to hold her tight to my chest to keep her quiet. She must have been a very agitated lass.

Televisions and radios could be heard. Some people were already singing the midnight carol, 'O Holy Night', even though it was barely ten. But these noises off were like an unreal soundtrack: the only real noise came from the rhythmic tap of our heels on wet pavement.

I was quite exhausted when she finally stopped in front

of a brand-new iron gate with a nameplate in yellow letters on a black background saying:

J. DRAVET & CO. — BINDERS

She took a key from her pocket and opened the gate. The moment of truth had come. I peered at the dark and mysterious area that lay behind the half-opened gateway. I could just about make out a yard with two lorries parked in it. At the back stood two-storey buildings whose large glazed roofs caught the light of the lamp-post at the street corner. Everything was black, new and silent.

We exchanged the same glance as we had in the cinema lobby.

"Right," she murmured, adding three perhaps very simple words that would nonetheless acquire a strange meaning later on:

"*This is it!*"

Was she taking her leave?

Or was she inviting me in?

It was simpler to ask her.

"Should I leave you here?"

She went on in without answering.

It was an invitation.

2

The First Visit

Under glazed awnings on both sides of the yard there were mountains of paper stacked up in reams.

At the rear stood the bindery. To the right was a wide iron door painted black with the word "Private" crudely stencilled on it.

The woman opened that door. She put her hand inside and turned a switch, but no light came on.

"That's right," she mumbled without any other explanation.

She took my arm and led me through the dark. I stumbled into the blackness like a blind man, terrified that I might bump the child's head into something.

My companion stopped. She fumbled around for a moment and then slid open the door of a lift.

"We're going to use the goods lift," she declared.

I followed her into a wide metal cage. Through its lattice ceiling, I could make out the faint gleam of a skylight two storeys above.

"You must be weary," she whispered in the dark. "She's heavy, isn't she?"

I could feel her hip against mine. I wished it would last all night.

The steel cage rose quite slowly. Then it jarred to a halt. My companion slid open the door and held it for me as I got out with the sleeping child.

"Mind the gap."

I took a long stride. She was holding my arm and her nails dug into my flesh. Presumably because she was worried I might drop the child?

It was pitch dark, because the narrow glass pane in the roof was directly above the lift shaft and didn't cast any light on the landing.

She needed a third key to open the front door of her dwelling.

This time the switch did its job. I found myself in a white-painted hallway. Glazed double doors opposite the entrance led to the lounge.

She led me in. The sequence of doors made me feel I was entering an unexpected labyrinth.

Why was I so stressed? What could be more reassuring than this young mother and her sleeping daughter? What more relaxing or soothing image could I hope for?

The room, which was painted white like the hallway, was not large, and a fair part of it was occupied by a Christmas tree. How many magic trees had I not already come across that day? It was a Christmas forest!

This one was decorated with real candles that gave it much more character than the strings of electric lights draped over the others. Modest decorations had been suspended from the tips of the branches.

"We had to move some furniture out because of the tree,"

the woman explained. "It must have looked quite a small tree in its native forest, but not here!"

What was left was a leather sofa, an armchair, a bar trolley and a gramophone on a low table.

"Do sit down and make yourself a drink! I'll put Lucienne to bed, it'll only take a few minutes. Do you like Wagner?"

She switched on the gramophone, adjusted the volume and gracefully took her daughter from me. She seemed to be waiting for something.

"So, what will you drink?"

"Well, that depends on what you've got to offer me," I bantered.

For the first time since I met the woman I managed not to look like a starved wolf.

"Oh, there's a bit of everything: cognac, whisky, cherry brandy…"

"In that case I'll have a cognac."

She hovered attentively. Why was she so keen for me to serve myself a drink? I didn't like serving myself. It was a bad habit Ma had given me. At home she always served everybody and when we had guests she sometimes grabbed their plates to stop them serving themselves.

"The cognac is the big bottle on the left."

I took it, then turned up a brandy glass that was standing upside down on a white doily. Hesitantly, I poured myself a measure.

It made her smile.

"You must excuse me."

"Of course."

She went out, closing the door behind her. I undid the buttons on my overcoat and, to fill the time, I stood up and went to look at the Christmas tree. A strange evening indeed!

I didn't know how far the affair would go, but it certainly was one!

When I put my hand in my pocket my fingers alighted on the edges of the little cardboard box containing the purchase I'd made that evening. Then it occurred to me that I could hang the silver-glittered birdcage with its blue and yellow bird on that tree. The thought made me feel really happy. God was smiling on me, on that Christmas night. Yes, the mere fact of unwrapping and attaching a cheap trinket to the prickly needles of a Christmas pine gave me a moment of pure joy.

I stepped back to admire the birdcage. I would not have felt prouder had I made it with my own two hands. It dangled on the end of the branch like a bell, sprinkling traces of its glitter-dust. The cloth bird rocked back and forth on its perch. I was looking at my own lost childhood with an unspeakable sense of wonder.

I squashed the cardboard box and put it back in my pocket. My tree offering had to stay secret so as to have a supernatural touch to it.

Perhaps my hostess and her daughter would never notice, but maybe they would find it and be puzzled no end.

I threw my coat on the sofa and picked up my glass of cognac. I hadn't drunk the stuff for a very long time. This was a top-class brand. The first sip gave me a feeling of euphoria. A dose of happiness!

The lady of the house came back after fifteen minutes. What surprised me was that she was still wearing her astrakhan coat. She followed my eyes and seemed to understand.

"That poor mite was so sleepy!" she said as she took off her coat.

Then she went to the drinks trolley.

"Let's see, what will I have? Cointreau, perhaps? Or a cherry brandy?"

She spoke up, because the music at that point was all trumpets and cymbals.

I watched her with secret admiration. I liked her gracefulness and ease. She had simple and expressive gestures that weren't put on at all. For me it was a magical experience to see her moving around the room, pouring herself a drop of cherry brandy, raising her glass in a silent toast and wetting her lips with the beetroot-coloured beverage.

My shoulder ached from carrying her daughter so far. To ease the discomfort I let my arms hang loose.

She went and turned down the volume on the gramophone.

"Do you live near here?"

"Yes, I do. But I've been away for six years, and I only came back this afternoon."

"That must be emotional for you, especially on Christmas Eve!"

Her voice was calm, with a rather flat intonation. It matched her body language perfectly.

"Did you come back because it was Christmas?"

"No. It just turned out that way."

"Were you far away?"

"Yes, a long way away."

The record came to an end. She switched the machine off and there was silence. She could feel I was reticent and held back from asking me questions. Yet I wanted to be interrogated. I was happy to talk as long as I didn't have to start the conversation. I needed some kind of priming.

"Isn't there anyone expecting you for the midnight ceremony?"

"No, nobody. I was on my own, as you were. And you noticed, didn't you?"

She looked away.

"I did."

Then, after a moment's thought:

"I would like to…"

"You would like what?"

"To dispense with any misunderstanding that my… my behaviour might have aroused…"

She was finding it hard to say what she meant and she seemed extremely embarrassed.

"What misunderstanding?"

"Well, I suppose that when a gentleman sits down in a cinema next to a lady he doesn't know and when that gentleman takes the lady's hand and the lady doesn't withdraw it, he must imagine he's just made an easy conquest."

I shook my head.

"It wasn't easy for me to take your hand, and you didn't find it easy to let me do so."

She drank a drop of cherry brandy, daintily.

"I don't suppose you'll believe me if I tell you that it's the first time anything like that has happened to me?"

"Why should I not believe you on a night that is spent celebrating a miracle?"

She threw me one of her devastatingly strange, sweet smiles.

"Thank you. I liked your taking my hand… I was in such distress."

"Me too!"

"Would you like to tell me about it?"

"Oh, my troubles are very much inside of me. If I put them into words, they lose their mystery and their power, you know…"

"Have a go, all the same."

"Seven years ago I'd just got my engineering diploma from technical school and landed a decent job when a great misfortune befell me."

"What kind of misfortune?"

"I fell in love."

"That could have been a great joy, couldn't it?"

"I thought it would be. At the beginning, it actually was. Only she was married, and what's more, married to my boss… We ran away. I left everything behind—my aged mother who'd slaved away so I could go to college, and my job, and the whole bang shoot!"

"And then?"

I'd not said a word about Anna to anyone for years. Long-buried images rose to the surface. I could see Anna in our hotel bed with one breast visible outside her nightgown. Or Anna with her hair in the wind by the seaside. Anna laughing! Anna crying! Anna dead!

"She died."

"Oh! Yes, that must have been dreadful."

"Yes, it was awful. After that I… went away."

"I understand."

"And while I was away Ma died too. The world has become a cemetery without any crosses for me now, it's full of graves and ghosts. And today I came back to this wasteland. I went back to our little flat round the corner from here. Instead of a Christmas tree there was just a sprig of holy palm in a glass that had once been full of holy water. I couldn't take it and went out. And I saw you in the restaurant with your daughter. You will always represent life for me."

"What you're telling me is very beautiful. To be able to be for someone else what one so rarely is for oneself is a great comfort."

I held out my hand towards her and she put hers in it. This time it wasn't frightened fingers pressing each other in the dark, it wasn't a liberty taken, but a deliberate act, more a gesture of human solidarity than a stolen caress.

"Tell me about yourself, now that we're swapping stories…"

"I'm from the other side."

"Meaning?"

"The side of the man whose wife you took."

She stopped talking. I was eager to learn more but I didn't dare rush her into a confession. She stared at my hand for a moment. I was ashamed because I no longer had middle-class hands.

"For me, it's seven years as well! I was a fine art student. I wanted to be a cinema set designer. I met the man who later became my husband. He was very handsome and he

32

was rich, he had a sports car that impressed me a lot. Girls of today often marry motorcars! It's a sickness of our age! I thought he was bringing me paradise on the chrome-plated luggage rack of his Jaguar. When he asked me to marry him I didn't say yes—I yelled it out loud! His family made a bit of a fuss because I didn't have any capital. My father is a retired army officer. When the Dravets learned that Papa had the right to wear his uniform at the wedding, they gave us the thumbs-up. A colonel in full dress really adds something to a wedding!"

She fell silent again as if she was letting her memories come back to her. Then it hit me again the way it had done in the cinema: I wanted to tell her I loved her.

"Since it's Christmas, may I tell you that I love you?"

"Oh, yes, you may! You may! Nobody has said that to me for a long time."

"Go on."

"You're interested in my story?"

"It's not a story."

"No," she muttered. "Hardly that. So I got married to that fine lad. His parents built him this bindery. Then Lucienne came along…"

"You too could have been very happy."

"I could. Only there's always something out of gear in real life, and that's what ruins it. The snag for you was the fact that you were in love with your boss's wife."

"And the snag for you?"

"It came from the fact that Lucienne was born six months after we got married and seven months after my first encounter with Jérôme. And she was the prettiest baby in the maternity ward. And in no need of an incubator," she added with bitter humour.

Her story was as classic as mine but much less romantic. She sighed.

"In business circles you don't make light of that kind of thing!"

"Divorce?"

"Catholic businessmen don't divorce."

"You hadn't… er… warned your fiancé about your… expectations?"

"No. I hadn't… Why am I telling you about such horrid things? I didn't expect to have my expectations, if you see what I mean. Before I met Jérôme I'd undertaken… Oh, let's use the polite words: I underwent a procedure. I'm telling you, it's utterly sordid."

"And then?"

"High drama. My in-laws would have nothing to do with me. And my husband lost interest in me very quickly, if that's not an understatement. At the beginning it wasn't too bad, he went with other women. But one day there was only one other woman, and my life became sheer torture. I hardly see him any more. He comes to the downstairs to look after his business. When he comes up here, it's to slap Lucienne or to call me a whore."

She poured me a serious measure of cognac and served herself another drop of cherry brandy.

"It's an odd kind of Christmas Eve, isn't it?" she went on. "We met an hour ago. I don't know your name and you know only my husband's. Yet we've just told each other our life stories straight off."

"Excuse me. My name is—"

Her hand shot up to cover my mouth.

"Please, no, don't tell me your name. It's so much better not to know. We've got time… Now I'd like to ask you for something…"

"Whatever you like."

"Let's go out! The kid's asleep, and she's a heavy sleeper. I can take a chance on leaving her alone for an hour or two. I'd like to go out on a man's arm and watch Christmas happening."

"On any man's arm?" I sighed.

She was enchanted.

"Heavens above! That's jealousy speaking. Do you see, that's probably what I miss the most: the jealousy…"

She was about to say something like "the jealousy of a man" but stopped herself in time and burst out laughing.

"Will you come?"

She picked up the glass I'd put on the mantelpiece and returned it to the top shelf of the drinks trolley. She must have been a good housekeeper and a natural tidier-up. She switched off the lights in the lounge and the hall. We were back in the dark on the landing.

"The bulb went two days ago," she said.

She took me by the hand and opened the door of the goods lift. She didn't let go all the way down. I liked the odd feeling of being swallowed that I always get from a lift cage going down.

The streets were quiet now. The sky was clearing and the night gleamed like burnished metal because of the frost. The shop windows were dark. Now and again groups of partygoers emerged from side streets forcing themselves to keep on laughing.

We walked arm in arm, at a gentle and happy pace, along empty streets that now looked immense.

The illuminated face of a street clock showed it was now ten forty. We came across a drunken beggar who asked me for a handout.

"Do you yourself believe that the night of Christmas Eve is not a night like any other?" she asked me.

"Of course I do, because that's what people have decided."

"You aren't a believer, then?"

"It comes and goes. I'm the opposite of other people. I believe when I am happy."

"Are you a believer at the moment?"

"Yes."

She was leaning on me heavily. I could feel her womanly warmth spreading through my body. A troubling desire for her had been nagging me ever since we started walking side by side, with our hips brushing each other.

At one point I felt a shiver go through her.

"Are you cold?"

"A bit."

"Do you want to go into a bar?"

"I don't want to see anybody."

It struck me all of a sudden: none of this made any sense. In my mind I flew way up and looked down on the area as if it were a matchstick model of a new town.

In it there was the woman's flat with a little girl asleep inside; my own mournful and desolate dwelling… And the

freezing streets we were moving along like sleepwalkers...
Suddenly she stopped.

"I'd like you to take me to your place."

I wasn't entirely surprised.

"I don't dare."

"Why?"

"Because it's horrible and it's been empty for so long."

"Doesn't matter. I'd like to see for myself."

"See what?"

"Does it bother you?"

"It does, actually, but if you insist..."

So we turned down my street. It was extremely unappealing and less well lit than other streets in the area. A dog padded contentedly along the pavement opposite, seemingly knowing where he was going, and stopped ceremoniously here and there to sniff at a wall.

"Here we are," I said as we stopped in front of a block of flats.

Its peeling façade looked like an ill-healed scorch mark. The main door was still open and a sneaky, foul-smelling draught blew through the porch.

I fumbled for the timer switch on the hallway light. I'd lost the habit of doing things like that. A twenty-year-old knack had been blunted by prolonged absence.

"No, don't switch on the light," she pleaded. "It's more mysterious in the dark."

We climbed the wooden staircase that had a carpet only up to the first floor. The middle part of it was worn down to the cord. On the next flight our feet trod on bare wood and sounded like drums. The steep balustrade was slightly sticky to the touch. I was as ashamed of it as I was of the smell of bleach that stung our nostrils.

In the old days when I had to open my own door after the timer had put the stair light out I would get the key straight into the hole out of sheer habit. But it took me a good two minutes to find it that night.

A yellow glass light fitting shaped like an upturned urn lit our hallway. It was attached to the ceiling by three plaited ropes ending in bobbles. The spiders had had it all to themselves. The wallpaper had buckled with the damp.

"Hasn't anybody been looking after the place since your mother died?"

"Yes, the stair lady, but she hasn't done it very well, as you can see."

I showed my companion into the dining room.

"A slice of life, right?" I joked as I nodded towards the few sticks of furniture, the brass pot-holders, the embroidered napkins, the check-patterned curtains, the beaded lampshades and the awful reproductions on the walls.

She didn't respond.

I showed her the oval table on which stood my mother's pride and joy, a statuette of an athlete with inordinately large muscles straining to push a cartwheel forward. The wheel was utterly absurd. As was the athlete, who seemed to be straining himself to the utmost for no good reason.

"There you are," I said. "I used to do my homework on this table because we ate all our meals in the kitchen, except on special occasions. For years I thought this was in very good taste. Then one day I realized, and I felt a bit ashamed. All the same I still liked the décor. Mainly because it gave me a sense of security that I've now lost forever."

There were tears in her eyes. I pushed her towards the room where Ma had died. I didn't have to explain, she understood. She stared at that painful place where I was still trying to find the shadow of a loved one.

She took the initiative and dragged me on to my bedroom.

"Will you go on living here?"

"I don't know."

"Do you have any plans?"

"I expect I'll go away. Only first I want to try and stay here for a while. Because of my mother, you understand? She died here alone because I was away. I'm going to try and make up for that by living here alone when she is away."

My voice cracked and yet I had thought it was steady enough. I put my head to the wall and pushed my clenched fists into my eyes as hard as I could.

A neighbour's radio was playing 'Come Back to Sorrento'.

The woman put her hands around my shoulders and nestled her head in my back.

"Tell me your first name, after all," she whispered.

3

The Outing

She went over to my bed and sat down.

She kept repeating my name in an undertone: "Albert… Albert…"

Seeing her sitting on the bed with her overcoat unbuttoned I realized she was the first woman ever to come into my room, and I think I blushed.

"It's strange how much you look like the woman I loved."

"Really?"

"Maybe it's clumsy of me to tell you that at a time like this."

She waved her arm vaguely to say, "Doesn't matter."

"What was she like?" Mme Dravet asked.

"Like I said: like you. A little less dark and slightly taller. But the shape of the face was the same and her eyes were like yours, intense and thoughtful."

"Was it because of the resemblance that you took an interest in me?"

"No."

"Do you still love her?"

The question upset me. I'd never asked it of myself since Anna's death.

"However strong your feeling may be for someone who's gone, it can't be called love."

I slid to my knees on the moth-eaten rug. I hugged her legs with fervour and her long-fingered and dainty hand moved towards my face to stroke it with gentle sadness.

"You'll always be a shy little boy, Albert!"

"Why?"

"I don't know why, I just know."

I let go of her legs and took her hand. I brought it to my lips. She had delicate, silky skin that was enchantingly cool.

"The prettiest hand in the world," I stammered.

She smiled with contentment.

"I'm glad you noticed my hands. Usually, men don't talk to women about their hands."

That was the moment when she noticed two tiny reddish spots shaped like stars on the edge of her cuff. They were set some distance apart and though they were really small they stood out clearly on the light fabric of her dress sleeve.

"What are those stains?" she muttered, realizing I had seen them too.

I laughed.

"Can you really call those pinpricks stains?"

My jokey tone didn't reassure her. She was really bothered. It doesn't take much to wreck a state of grace. I realized with dismay that ours had suddenly ended. Seconds before the incident with the dress, we'd been floating in a slightly unreal world. The woman was already mine. Everything we'd been saying, everything we'd been doing, including when we were not saying anything, was leading us to the logical conclusion of physical love.

And then it was over. The charm was broken. Back to where

we began: at a loss and on our own, infinitely alone, on this strange Christmas night.

"I'd like some water to try and get rid of the stain."

Our flat didn't have a bathroom. For twenty years I'd washed at the kitchen sink. So I took her to the kitchen. But the water had been switched off, despite the fact that I'd written to the housekeeper to keep on paying the service charges. When I turned on the tap, not a single drip came out.

My companion seemed distressed.

"Come on," I sighed. "Let's go to a bar."

And that's why we left the flat. As I watched her walk out the door it struck me that but for a moment's silence I would have been holding her in my arms. The disappointment was physically painful, as if my whole body were sorry for itself.

As a young man, how many times had I dreamed that I was lying with a woman in my bachelor's bed? Never the same one twice, of course. I adorned my imaginary partners with faces I'd come across during the day: a salesgirl who'd smiled at me, a smart lady I'd watched on the sly as she got out of a car, or simply an actress featured on a magazine cover…

Years too late, but in a manner far more magical than in my teenage dreams, I'd just missed making them come true.

"Are you feeling down?" she observed as we were sauntering once again along empty streets.

"Yes, a bit."

"Why, Albert?"

"Please don't call me Albert."

"Don't I say it right?"

"No."

I wasn't being rude, I only meant to be honest.

"To say a man's name properly, you have to be in love."

"You sound resentful."

"I am."

"Why?"

"I think it's not fair that I should have feelings for you that you don't share."

"Who says I don't?"

"I can tell. Love at first sight, the real thing, that only happens to men. Women are much too sensible to soar to the heights of love in a few minutes."

She stopped in her tracks.

"Kiss me," she said.

It was almost a command. She sounded determined, and fierce.

I took her by the waist and squashed my lips on hers. Her kiss drove me quite insane.

When our lips parted we started walking again, very fast, like people who are scared.

"You wanted to do it just now, in your bedroom, didn't you?"

"Yes."

"And you are a bit cross with me?"

"Not any more. It was better this way."

She shrugged.

"Of course it is better this way. Only a man could think the opposite."

We were outside a big café that was packed. We went in and stood at the bar because all the tables were taken. A jukebox thumped away. Young people in their Sunday best and paper hats blew toy trumpets in time with the music.

At the back of the premises four old guys were playing cards. On Christmas Eve! Unbelievable!

"Excuse me for a minute."

With her airy stride she wound her way through the boozers towards the toilets. I ordered a very strong coffee and filled the time waiting for her by watching the way the lighting of the jukebox changed colour. The record rotated vertically like a grinding wheel, and the pickup arm was shaped like a piston.

"There we are, all mended!"

She was showing me the wetted edge of her cuff.

"So what was it?"

"Splashes from a red candle."

Her claim was vaguely shocking. I'd seen the two stains. I knew full well they weren't candle wax.

"What'll you have?"

"Nothing. I have to go back now. Don't forget my daughter is on her own."

By moonlight the premises of Dravet & Co. looked like a set of toy cubes. Soot hadn't yet dulled the walls and the white roughcast stood out clearly in the December night.

"Well, then," Mme Dravet sighed, "this is where we part. What time is it?"

I looked at my watch.

"Eleven forty-five."

"In fifteen minutes the son of God will be born again. Do you think he'll redeem all the world's sins in the end?"

I suddenly felt so sad I wanted to die.

"I don't give a damn for the world's sins, Mme Dravet. I don't give a damn for the world! All I'm interested in is you. I'm sick as a dog to think we'll not see each other again…"

"But we will!"

"In another life?" I grunted.

"Don't be unfair. Do you want to come and have a last drink before the bells ring out?"

To stay with her a little more! To see her a little more! To hear her a little more!

"Yes, yes and yes!"

She opened the gloomy gate once more. I was back in the yard with the lorries parked against the wall, with the glazed awnings sheltering mountains of paper, and the smell of glue and cardboard.

"What kinds of things does your binder bind? Books?"

"Yes. But most of all he produces diaries."

When we got into the goods lift again she abruptly pressed herself against me and as the steel cage rose she gave me a kiss that was just as hot and passionate as the first one.

The machinery had come to a halt but we were still in a wild embrace. She slid one of her legs between mine; I was hugging her tightly. Our breaths and our mouths were one.

"Come," she said suddenly, as she pushed me away from her.

Her gesture was so violent it gave me a shock. She opened the sliding door and repeated almost automatically what she'd said the other time:

"Mind the gap."

4

The Second Visit

We went into her flat as quietly as we could so as not to wake the sleeping child. Only once we were inside and the front door was closed did she switch on the light. Then she cried out. It wasn't exactly a scream, it was more like a moan.

"What's the matter?" I stuttered in concern.

She was staring at the coat rack in the hallway. A dark grey overcoat with a velvet collar was hanging on it.

The coat had not been there when we went out.

It mesmerized her. She was holding her breath and straining her ears as if to make out from the quality of the silence the nature of the threat hanging over us.

For threat there was!

I felt it so surely that I lost all sense of fright.

"Is it your husband's?" I whispered.

She nodded.

"So 'he' is here?"

I was about to say something more but she put her hand over my mouth in double-quick time. She persisted in listening. What was worrying was the coat on the hook and the complete lack of sound in the flat.

I took her hand away and kept it in mine as if to inspire courage in her. I could hear her heart thumping. I mouthed the syllables with my lips so she could understand me without my speaking aloud:

"Was he not supposed to come back?"

She shook her head.

"Maybe he came for a change of clothes and went away again?"

She shrugged. Doubtful.

"He must have gone to bed?"

Only the sibilant in my speech made any sound. I must have looked like a mute. But even deaf mutes make a noise!

She shook her head again.

What seemed to disturb the woman was not so much that the man might be dangerous, but that his presence was so unusual.

"Should I leave?"

I was afraid of looking like a coward by offering to go away. Suitors who slip away when the husband turns up are creeps. In any case I had no wish to run away.

I was entirely prepared to face the anger of a jealous man. I had plenty of unused energy inside me that wanted nothing better than a chance to be let out.

She dithered. I could understand her being in a muddle. She wasn't sure what she wanted. Should we run away or stand our ground?

She made her decision abruptly. In an almost firm voice she called out:

"Is that you, Jérôme?"

No answer! The ensuing silence was as sharp as a prick on a taut nerve.

I shrugged.

"I told you he's gone away. He didn't find you at home, so he decided to spend the rest of the evening somewhere else…"

This time I spoke aloud.

The woman batted her eyelids in acceptance of my guess. The lights were out in the lounge, so there was nobody there. She went down the corridor, opening each door in turn. One went into her daughter's bedroom, so that's where she started. I moved forward and saw little Lucienne sleeping soundly in a little bed made of a light-coloured wood. There were plywood Donald Ducks on the wall and toys strewn on the carpet.

The door opposite the girl's was the main bedroom. There was nobody in it. The bed was not unmade. It was a four-poster with two turned-wood columns at the foot and an extremely ornate valance.

"You can see nobody's here!"

Just to make sure, she took a quick look at the kitchen and the dining room.

Nobody there either!

She began to seem calmer.

"I don't understand why he came in the middle of the night. It's not like him at all…"

"Maybe he wanted to wish you a happy Christmas?"

"Him? You obviously don't know him. Well, it's a real mystery… Let's have a drink. It's nearly midnight."

I grabbed her by the waist.

"It *is* midnight!"

I put my finger in the air.

"Listen!"

A local clock chimed twelve times, slowly. Its low pitch sent vibrations through the still night air.

"Kiss me!" she suddenly pleaded. "I'm scared!"

I took her in my arms.

"Harder! Harder! I'm scared…"

She was agitated in the extreme. She pressed herself up against me so frantically that I too got scared.

"There, there, calm down. Scared of what? I'm here…"

She opened the French door to the lounge and switched on the light.

It was a dreadful sight. The man lay half-reclining on the sofa where I had sat on my first visit. He had one leg on the cushions and his back against the armrest. He was wearing a midnight blue suit. His left hand hung loose, and his right hand was all scrunched up between his cheek and the back of the sofa. Part of his skull was missing. From his right temple to the top of his head there was nothing but a bloody mess. The bullet had shattered the skull and then hit the ceiling, knocking out a lump of plaster.

The dead man had his eyes closed. In his half-open mouth you could see the gleam of a gold front tooth.

The woman said nothing. She reminded me of a sapling that's had its trunk cut through by an axe but doesn't topple over straight away. I quickly grabbed her by the shoulders to push her back into the hallway.

She was dreadfully pale and her chin was quivering.

She stared at the coat on the hook as if it were the corpse itself.

"That your husband?" I asked her eventually in an almost inaudible whisper.

"Yes."

You could hear people far away singing 'O Holy Night'. The song came from outer space the way the wind comes from the infinite.

You caught snatches, then suddenly it got louder.

I went back into the little lounge. The cadaver by the Christmas tree was nightmarish. The man was thirty-two or thirty-three with fairly refined features. His slightly jutting square jaw showed he was a man of action.

I carefully made my way around the sofa. I didn't want to touch anything, just to get a full view. I saw the gun lying between the man's chest and the back of the sofa. He'd let go of it as he died.

He'd been dead for a while. Probably since just after we'd left. He'd lost a lot of blood and it was all over the cushions. I looked around for a note explaining what had led him to do away with himself but there wasn't one. Maybe it would be found later, in his clothes…

A slight noise made me turn around. I saw the woman in the doorway leaning her head on the jamb. She was staring at her deceased husband more in disbelief than in fear.

She did not understand.

"Is he really dead?" she asked me.

"Yes."

It was a superfluous question. When a man has a hole in his head as big as that one was, it's pretty obvious he's ceased to exist.

Why the hell did it occur to him to commit suicide in front of that tree of joy, which is a hymn to life?

The drinks trolley was still beside the sofa. And our two glasses were still on it, containing, respectively, a last drop of cherry brandy and a smear of cognac.

"This is dreadful," Mme Dravet murmured as she went up to the corpse.

"Don't touch him!" I urged her. "It's very important."

"Ah yes… Because of the police."

"That's right, because of the police. In suicides of this kind the tiniest detail can be of the utmost importance…"

"Suicide?"

"He shot himself in the head, can't you see?"

She really seemed not to believe it.

For a moment we were in suspension. We knew there were things to do but we were finding it hard to behave sensibly.

I wondered what she really felt. Was she sorry? I almost asked her, but with the corpse lying there it wasn't possible.

"We have to call the police."

"Of course we do."

But she didn't make a move. The dead man's wound fascinated her.

Everything had happened dead fast. Proof of that was that the church bell we'd already heard was still chiming midnight. As brief as a nightmare! You dream of scary adventures, you struggle out of innumerable traps, and then suddenly you realize that the fantasy has lasted no longer than it takes to blink! Only for us, it would go on. The corpse was a real corpse that we carried on staring at because now and again we thought we saw something stir in this abandoned body! We were just fooling ourselves. We were waiting for the bad dream to be over, but it wasn't a dream. Reality outwaits us all.

At last Mme Dravet reacted and rushed out of the room. I could hear her going down the corridor. A minute later I could hear the ratchet of the telephone dial. Then something awful occurred to me. Something that had not occurred to me before.

I shot out of the lounge like a lunatic. She was in her bedroom sitting on a pouf with the phone in her lap. She had just finished dialling when I snatched the phone from her.

The receiver went flying onto the dressing table where it broke a perfume bottle. The room filled instantly with the penetrating odour of tuberose.

The young woman seemed in a panic.

"But why…?"

"Wait a moment before you talk to the police."

The rest of what I had to say was not easy!

"But I have to, all the same," she protested.

"Yes, you do have to. Only you cannot tell the cops about me! I cannot be mixed up in this kind of a business."

She was downhearted but her mind remained clear. I saw a flash of scorn in her eyes. I had suddenly turned into a miserable skirt-chaser who had no wish to get entangled and who was scared out of his wits at the complications it would bring.

"I know what you are thinking, but you are wrong. I'm asking you to leave me out for your own protection. My presence in your flat tonight can do you a lot of harm. I am very far from being an acceptable alibi."

She had almost stopped breathing. With her lips open a slit and her eyes agog she looked like she might faint any minute. Her catatonic state alarmed me.

"Do you feel sick?"

"No. Tell me more."

Tell more! That was so hard, after what had just happened!

"I told you my story earlier this evening. But not all of it. The rest of it is untellable…"

I stopped talking. In exasperation she started screaming at me:

"Tell me! You can see I can't take any more!"

"The woman I ran away with… Three months later she'd cooled off and wanted to leave me… So I… I killed her! I had an emotional breakdown! That's what my lawyer called it, anyway. I was tried in Aix-en-Provence and got ten years… Yesterday I was released from the Baumettes prison in Marseilles, I got remission."

I said that all in one go without looking at her. I kept my eyes on the phone on the floor. It looked like a dead animal. I picked it up and put the receiver back in the cradle.

"I'm an ex-con, Mme Dravet. If the police know that we spent part of the evening together, your husband's suicide is going to look suspicious, you see. I know the cops! They're always inclined to put the worst interpretation on things."

She put her head in her hands. Her nightmare wasn't over. It was acquiring strange sequels.

"On the other hand," she muttered, "we can't be suspects. We were together. We didn't spend any time apart."

"Who says so? You do and I do. If the police thought we were in cahoots we'd be in a fine pickle. Mud sticks. I've already killed someone, don't you see!"

She gave me a look full of fear and shrank away from me. That woman had just taken on board that I was a murderer and she was feeling what everybody feels in like circumstances: fear and repulsion.

"Get out!"

"All right…"

"Leave this flat immediately!" she thundered.

"Perhaps we should first agree on—"

"No! I don't know you! Once you're out that door I will never have set eyes on you, do you get it?"

"As you wish. Only the police—"

"I'll take care of them. Go away!"

I went out of the room backwards, alarmed by her evil stare. In the two or three hours we'd spent together I thought she was weak and lost but now, all of a sudden, she had turned strangely cold and decisive in adversity. She wasn't behaving at all like a victim any more. Her whole being expressed a lack of pity, which was quite painful to me. I tried to recall the affectionate pout she put on when I first took her in my arms.

It wasn't the same woman.

I sobered up completely in the hallway.

There was a dead man in this flat. I was in the same place without a reason I could own up to, and I was just out of jail!

I realized the flat was nothing but a skein of snares. I was on my way out when I remembered my cognac glass standing less than two feet from the corpse. It must have had first-rate samples of my fingerprints all over it.

I went back into the lounge to clean the glass with my handkerchief. I also wiped the neck of the squat cognac bottle, and then to make doubly sure I wiped the rim of the drinks trolley and the marble shelf of the mantelpiece. Finally, I dusted the handle of the lounge door.

As I was putting my handkerchief back in my coat pocket my fingers encountered the crumpled cardboard box that had contained the tree decoration. I had almost missed it! I didn't think fingerprints would have taken on such a rough surface but it was wiser to leave nothing behind.

I went up to the tree. I was stretching out my arm to remove the little silver cage but it froze in mid-air as if I'd been struck with paralysis: the cage and its cloth bird had vanished.

I parted the branches of the tree to see if it had perhaps fallen off, but however much I looked there was nothing to be found. *Someone had removed it.*

I heard Mme Dravet's footsteps in the hallway.

"Still not gone?" she said in surprise.

She looked at me with suspicion. She glanced at my hands, then at her husband's corpse. Was she worried I might have shifted something?

She looked more and more like Anna. She had the same blank stare that was Anna's when she told me it was "all over between us" and that she wanted to go back to her husband.

All the same I would have liked to hold her in my arms again and offer soothing words.

"Excuse me. I'm leaving now."

She opened the front door for me. I think she mumbled adieu but I'm not sure.

5

A Piece of Advice

The door slammed shut behind me and I found myself in darkness. A piercing smell of glue wafted up from downstairs. I struck a match to see where I was going. To my left was the stairwell and straight ahead was the goods lift.

I went into the steel cage. It was long and narrow like a hospital lift, designed to carry people lying on stretchers.

I looked for the control panel. The match was nearly burned down to my finger. I could see two switches: a black one and a red one. Red was at the top, black below. That's the one I pressed. The lift cage gave an electric shudder and began to go down very gently. I dropped the match, which burned itself out on the floor. A tiny slip of white paper caught fire and I put it out with the sole of my shoe. The faint gleam of light vanished.

On seeing the two lorries parked in the yard I wondered about Dravet's own car. Surely he hadn't come home on foot? And if not, then what had become of his car? I looked around but I couldn't see it anywhere. Nor was it to be found in the street. Had someone dropped him off? Was that someone the same person who had removed my silver-spangled cardboard cage?

The object's disappearance worried me almost more than the death of the binder.

I paced up and down with my fists clenched angrily in my coat pockets. I resented humankind's lack of mercy. After six years mouldering in prison, after exhausting my capacity for remorse, after sleeplessness that was worse than a nightmare, I'd been kicked back into a bloody drama. Anna died because of my own despair, but her end hadn't cured me of it. I wasn't free of the shadow of death. In six years, I'd had just two hours of oblivion with Mme Dravet. They didn't add up to much.

I should have fled the area and got as far away as possible while other people's celebrations went on roaring like a brazier.

But an invisible force kept me prowling round the house. I could not accept such a bizarre situation. I could not allow myself to leave the woman to whom I owed what was perhaps the high point of my life all on her own between a sleeping daughter and her husband's corpse. All there'd been between us were two kisses that we both knew would lead nowhere, but they had brought us together more solidly than any wild embrace—more permanently than a legal marriage, and more powerfully than a sacrament.

She'd virtually thrown me out. She had the harsh look of a woman who will not forgive the man she fancies for having deceived her. I'd let her down by being unable to help her. She'd understood that her own interests required me to remove myself; she'd understood, but not accepted it.

There was a building site behind a slatted fence on the opposite side of the street. Giant cranes and pyramids of construction materials made this former piece of wasteland look like a port. Abutting the fence was a bus stop with a glazed-in shelter. I slipped into this hut-like refuge. I put up the collar of my coat and sat down on the stone bench.

I meant to wait not too far away from her to see what would happen next. She might even need me. I couldn't foresee in what way, but I felt it intuitively. The police would be coming. They would make their observations. How would Mme Dravet extricate herself from what was a pretty bad situation? She couldn't claim to have stayed at home and not heard the bang! On the other hand if she said she'd gone out the cops would ask her where she had gone, and that was something she couldn't tell them either... Unless... Of course! The idea was a good one!

I left the shelter and dashed to the nearest café. It wasn't the one where we'd been a little while before, but a coalman's dive which for once was staying open very late that night.

All it had were three tables and a small bar. The narrow room had been divided into two, and in the other half you could buy packs of charcoal and bundles of firewood.

The barman and his wife were seeing in Christmas with half a dozen regulars. On the table was a pan of fried blood sausage that gave off a wholesome smell of hot butter.

The partygoers had drunk too much and weren't talking. They seemed almost sad.

They looked at me as if I were an intruder.

"Telephone, please!"

The short, fat barman, who had a moustache and a nose that looked like it was made of toad skin, sighed as he stood up with his napkin in his hand.

"Shop next door."

He showed me to it and stood there quite shamelessly waiting for me to finish, picking his teeth all the while with the tip of a knife.

Before leaving the bus shelter I'd seen the Dravets' telephone number painted on the nameplate on the yard gate. I dialled as fast as I could, but since I'd been in prison I'd lost among many other habits the knack of using a telephone dial. I had to try it several times over.

At last I could hear the phone ringing at the other end. Heavens above! As long as the police weren't already on the case!

The ring tone went on and on with manic regularity. Just as I was about to give up in despair, someone picked up but didn't make a sound, not even the mechanical and instinctive "Hello!"

My throat was dry. No two ways about it: that was an officer on the end of the line. I knew how the police went about things…

My mind was racing so fast I felt dizzy. What should I do? Keep silent? That would seem suspicious. Pretend I'd dialled a wrong number? I didn't feel up to bluffing. I was bound to put my foot in it.

"It's me," I blabbed pitifully.

Mme Dravet's voice was sweet music to my ears.

"I thought so. What do you want?"

"Are you alone?"

"Yes."

"Did you call…?"

"The police are on their way."

"I thought, I think... Well, you could say you went to Midnight Mass to explain why you were out."

"Mind your own business. I must ask you very firmly not to contact me again by any means whatsoever."

She hung up.

The moustachioed coalman had finished cleaning his teeth.

The café diners were trying to start a conversation but their tongues were so thick they could hardly articulate.

"Eugène!" the bar lady called out. "Your food will be cold."

"Coming."

He switched off the light in the second shop even before I was out of it. The diners stared at me strangely, with eyes bleary from red wine.

In the old days Ma and I had an odd way of celebrating Christmas. We would stay at home. I would lay out my set of chipped plaster figurines on the marble dresser to make a nativity scene. We would dine on cold chicken and a bottle of champagne and spend the evening by the wavering light of the big candles that we sometimes saved up for the following year...

"What will you have?"

I looked at the barman.

"Take off the door handle when you're done with the gentleman!" his wife instructed, with her mouth full.

"Brandy!"

He filled a glass barely bigger than a thimble. A pair of red wine splashes on the counter reminded me of the two tiny stains on Mme Dravet's cuff. I thought of her great hurry to get rid of them. I was now sure they were bloodstains. The idea worried me.

60

I paid and left without drinking the brandy. Only after I'd gone some paces along the street did I remember the thimbleful.

I went back automatically to the bus shelter to keep watch on the house on the other side of the street. There was no police car parked in front of J. Dravet & Co. Were the emergency services overstretched that night? Why were they taking so long? More than a quarter of an hour had gone by since I'd left the flat.

When I had first got to Mme Dravet's home with her daughter asleep in my arms, I'd felt a flash of anxiety. It was as if I were crossing the threshold of a mysterious labyrinth and pushing on into a weird and lightless maze. Now I had that feeling again, only with a stronger sense of it being real.

The big black gate with its yellow lettering was like the cover of a scary book telling the murky tale of the couple inside.

A woman on her own with her child on Christmas Eve. A husband turning up to kill himself in front of the Christmas tree.

Two spots of blood on a cuff. A decoration that vanishes from a branch of the tree…

And a fourth character: Me! I played what was after all an important part—the witness.

I jumped on hearing a slight grating noise. The factory gate was opening.

Mme Dravet in her astrakhan overcoat was going out, holding her daughter by the hand.

6

The Diversion

She closed the heavy gate behind her but did not lock it. She looked left and then right like someone who's not sure which way to go.

In fact, I think she was looking to see if I was there. I sensed it and squeezed into the darkest corner of the shelter. She was scared of coming face to face with me. From now on my wish to help her could only bring her harm.

The wakened child was whimpering as she trotted alongside her mother. Where could they be going? I suddenly feared that Mme Dravet had taken a fateful decision. Maybe it was the only way out that the woman could imagine? Maybe she had had enough of the struggle? When she'd dialled the emergency number she'd nearly fainted.

When I'd had Anna's lifeless body before my eyes, I too felt that my own life could not go on. I'd wanted to leave, to get off, like getting out of a moving car. That's why I put the smoking barrel of the gun between my teeth. But the smell of the gunpowder was asphyxiating, and I think a convulsive bout of coughing was the only thing that prevented me from going all the way.

The two silhouettes grew smaller as they made their way through the icy night. They were going towards the centre of town. Far beyond them, a luminous haze in the sky signalled Paris. I let them get some distance ahead of me before leaving my shelter.

They stopped from time to time. Mme Dravet leaned over her daughter to say something to her. Then they started off again, hesitantly. The mother walked slowly but the little girl still had to make an effort to keep up.

They crossed a deserted square and suddenly, seeing the looming mass of a church with light in its stained-glass window at the other side of the esplanade, I understood that the young woman was taking my advice. She was going to Midnight Mass. Instead of lying to the police, she was setting up a genuine alibi. That was much cleverer.

When I entered the building myself, the tinny bell was ringing for the elevation. The church was packed and I had to stand near the door, in the middle of a heap of worshippers. All their heads were bowed. I would have liked to try and pray too, but all my thoughts were with the woman lost in the crowd of churchgoers.

She was all that counted. She was playing a dire hand at this minute, and I felt ever more forcefully that I needed to help her. Taking advantage of the fact that everyone else was bowing down in devotion, I looked around. Mme Dravet was at the back of the main aisle. She was looking at the altar where the priest was holding up the host, and appeared to be in ecstatic communion. What was she actually thinking? Was she frightened of the danger hanging over her? Or was she thinking of when she had loved Jérôme Dravet? What was she asking of God? The salvation of her body, or of her soul?

Then the great organ expelled its inexhaustible, vibrating breath.

A huge rustling noise ran through the congregation—the sound of chairs and feet being shifted and shuffled. Then the choristers began to sing. Since some worshippers were already leaving the church, Mme Dravet moved up the aisle in search of a pew.

She slipped into a row not far from the pulpit and was lost to view.

I think I was then on the point of leaving myself. The heavenly peace of the church brought all the weariness of the day down on me and, even more, the weight of the emotions I'd had in the course of the evening. I needed a decent hotel room, preferably not facing the street. Ah! To be able to draw the curtains, drop onto a bed and pass out! I'd spent my first night of freedom on a train and I'd not got a wink of sleep because of the abrupt change of environment. The nightlight in the compartment reminded me of the light in my prison cell. Was I not still in a prison? A prison moving at seventy miles an hour, and with cellmates as depressing as those I'd had at Baumettes!

The service went on with flaming candles. Now everyone was singing to the birth of Jesus. I felt faint. I shifted from one foot to the other in an effort to overcome my fatigue. I was slightly dizzy.

Suddenly, as one hymn ended, the noise of a chair falling over echoed through the nave and then came the sound of a child crying. A foreboding made me look towards the pulpit. I saw there was some kind of to-do in that part of the church.

Then a small group emerged from the silent commotion and came down the aisle.

I felt like I'd just been punched in the chest! Two men were carrying a lifeless Mme Dravet towards the exit, and a lady was leading a weeping Lucienne by the hand.

When the procession drew level with me I dashed out. I was crazy with worry in case the woman had poisoned herself before coming here...

"What happened?" I asked one of the two men.

"She passed out."

We all went outside. Under the porch I looked at Mme Dravet and noticed the strange look in her eyes, under her long lowered eyelashes. They weren't the eyes of a woman who'd fainted. Quite the opposite, in fact. They were dreadfully alert.

"Do you know her?" the lady asked.

"Er... By sight. We live in the same area."

"We must take her home," one of the men decided. "If you would be so kind as to help my friend to keep her upright, I'll go and get my car which is parked round the corner."

The man who stayed behind with me must have been about fifty, and I quickly worked out that the woman who was looking after Lucienne was his wife.

"I was completely taken aback," he said. "She was sitting next to me. She put her hand to her forehead and then just keeled over... Do you think it's serious?"

Mme Dravet was pale and her nostrils were pinched. She was acting her part to perfection.

"I feel sorry for the wee mite," the lady confided.

She was stroking Lucienne's cheek as the child sniffled sorrowfully and looked all around her in a daze.

"The wee one went to sleep in church. When her mother fell over it woke her up…"

I was afraid the little girl might recognize me. But she had only set eyes on me at the restaurant, and hadn't paid me any special attention.

The man with the car came back at the wheel of a black Peugeot 403 and drew up at the foot of the church steps. He opened the rear door and motioned to us to come on down. As we were holding the pseudo-patient upright she let her head loll towards me and whispered:

"Keep away!"

Straight after, as we reached the car, she heaved a deep sigh and opened her eyes.

"Are you feeling better?" the sympathetic lady asked.

"What happened to me?"

"A turn. It was so hot in the church… We were next to a heating vent, in fact…"

"What about my daughter?"

"She's here. We'll drive you home."

"Thank you."

The husband then said to the driver of the Peugeot:

"Seeing as she's better and this gentleman is with you…"

He must have had a party on at his place or else chums to see.

"No problem," the driver conceded gladly. "Happy Christmas to you both!"

He was older than I was, maybe forty or so. He was tall and ruddy and wore a leather coat and a big woollen scarf. A likeable fellow, kind-hearted and practical without a doubt.

We got Mme Dravet and Lucienne onto the rear seat.

"Which way?" the man in the leather coat enquired.

"On the other side of the square, turn left."

Before switching on the engine he took a look at his passenger.

"Better?"

"Yes, thank you," she stammered.

My being in the car scared her stiff. I could easily undermine her plan of action.

"Wait a minute, I'll put your window down. Nothing like a spot of fresh air for cases of this kind," the helpful driver continued.

I was holding the little girl tight. The driver rounded a wide bend then put his foot down.

"Do you want to go see a medic?"

"It's not worth the trouble. Thank you all the same, you are most considerate…"

He shrugged and mumbled contentedly:

"If you say so…"

I felt physically sick when the dark gate with its bright lettering came into view once again. Back to square one. The young woman must have felt the same dizzying frustration. What right had I to intervene in her fate once again after she had sent me packing?

The leather-coated man got out of the driving seat and went round the car to help his passenger get out. As he passed in front in the yellow light of the headlamps she said without moving her head:

"Please, do me a favour and get lost!"

The man opened the car door and held out his large and helping hand.

"Gently does it. You think you'll be all right? Wouldn't you prefer to be carried by the two of us?"

"No, no. If you would just see me up to my flat."

"The least I could do!"

The big jolly fellow then gave me a salacious wink that suddenly filled me with an icy rage quite beyond my control.

"I'll prop her up. You look after the kid."

Mme Dravet couldn't stop looking at me with burning eyes. It was a look that contained everything—despair, fear, and anger as well.

I behaved as if I'd not seen her forceful glance.

I swept the girl into my arms with resolve.

We walked to the gateway.

It was starting a second time over.

7
The Third Visit

The bells were ringing out the end of the midnight service. Those happy chimes sounded nonetheless like a dirge, since I knew what was in store. I knew I would see the corpse a second time and would have to behave as if it were the first. What treacherous devil was propelling me back to this accursed place to act in the most dangerous of plays?

A short while before I'd had only one thing in mind, to relieve this house of my discreditable self so as to give Mme Dravet free rein. But now, against all caution and in breach of her pleas, I was imposing myself on the young woman. It was not logical. There was still time to invent an excuse and clear off. But still I went on across the courtyard.

"He's a binder, is he, your husband?"

"Yes."

"I'm in wallpaper. Not so very different, is it?"

We'd got to the door. The second door. I stepped ever on into the labyrinth.

"It's black as pitch in here…"

"The bulb went."

"I've got a lighter. Don't move. Hang on, I can see the stairs."

"No need. There's a goods lift…"

She opened the door and we went into the cage. The door made its characteristic swishing sound as it closed.

The leather-coated man asked in a tentative manner:

"Is there anyone at home?"

I was struck by this conventional question.

I envied the simple, peaceful voice of the man. He wasn't apprehensive in the least, he didn't have an inkling. He was uncomplicated and straight as a die. He probably loved his job, good fun, and his fellow man…

I was sorry to be in the dark. I would have liked to keep an eye on Mme Dravet. Would she be strong enough to play her game to the end?

She opened the flat door without a quiver. She led the way into the hall and switched on the light.

She was avoiding my eyes. She was a bit pale, to be sure, but didn't the man believe she'd just come out of a dizzy spell?

"I'll take you into the lounge," she said in a voice that was slightly flat but didn't waver.

I squeezed Lucienne's hand.

I would not allow myself to show the child the hideous scene that was lying in wait. Mme Dravet switched on the lounge light then moved back to let us go in too. I stood with my shoulders hunched waiting for the leather-coated man to scream in horror.

"Ah! What a lovely tree," he muttered as he stepped over the threshold of the lounge.

Then I pushed him aside to see more quickly for myself.

There was no longer any corpse in the room.

"Do sit down."

Her expression remained impenetrable, but all the same I thought I saw a faint smile flit across her face.

What had she done with her husband's body? She had perhaps lost the whole game by moving it. I resented her for having done anything so insane.

I glanced around to see if there were any traces of the tragedy. There was none. She had cleaned the leather sofa.

I then turned round to see if Dravet's overcoat was still hanging on the hook in the hall, but it was not. Obviously the woman had changed her tack. Where the hell could she have dragged the corpse? But if she'd planned on getting rid of it, why had she gone to church so as to pretend to faint at Midnight Mass?

I would have given ten years of my life to have a no-holds-barred talk with her.

"I'm extremely grateful to you gentlemen, you have been so considerate…"

"Don't mention it," the man in the leather coat assured her, for he was pleased to have done a good deed right in the middle of Christmas.

He must have been a believer since he went to church. He must surely have told himself that his good behaviour would add to his balance of eternal bliss.

"Do me a favour and have a drink while I put my daughter back to bed…"

"Can I lend you a hand?" I hurried to offer, since it would give me a chance to speak to her alone.

"Certainly not, thank you very much."

She sounded courteous, but her eyes were ice-cold.

71

"Sit down!"

The other man undid his leather coat and flopped onto the sofa. I felt a shiver go from the top of my head to my toes.

"What'll you have?"

She had washed up our glasses and had put them back in place in the metal glass-holder on the trolley.

"Whatever you like, but make it a stiff one," the car driver said.

"Cognac?"

"Sure."

"And yourself?"

I looked at her with all my soul. I wanted really badly to seize her by the waist, press her against me and say, "Stop this mad game, I'm going to help you. We'll try and sort it all out."

"Cognac for me too."

She poured our drinks for us. I settled into the small armchair as she dragged the sleepy little girl towards her bedroom.

The man sniffed his glass, then made a face to show he recognized and appreciated top-quality spirits.

"My name's Ferrie," he blurted out, suddenly concerned with the social niceties. "Not with a 'y', like the boats to England! I'm an 'ie': Paul Ferrie, at your service."

"Albert Herbin…"

He gave me his free hand. I found the situation grotesque.

"A lovely lady, isn't she?"

He jutted his chin towards the door.

"Very lovely, yes."

"As far as I can make out, her life's not a bed of roses."

"Why not?"

72

"Well, if her husband leaves her on her own on a night like this…"

"Maybe he's away on business?"

"Yes, maybe. But I don't know, she strikes me as sad, don't you think?"

This guy was my exact opposite. But he had the same feelings about Mme Dravet as I did. It touched me, it even disturbed me.

"A bit, that's true."

"Do you think she's pregnant?"

"Whatever made you think of that?"

"Well, the way she passed out!"

"It would be tricky to ask her," I muttered.

Ferrie shrugged and then downed his cognac.

"Mine's in hospital right now, with a big baby boy two days old. If he'd waited a bit longer he would have been baby Jesus! We took a long time having him. We'd lost hope, and then, you see… And that's why our Christmas is a bit chaotic this year. My wife is very devout and she insisted I go to Midnight Mass in her stead. Religion's not my strong point, but for the sake of the baby…"

Like any happy man he needed to tell people about himself. The shot of spirits made him even keener to spill his beans. He didn't even notice I was hardly listening to him.

"Are you married?"

"No."

"You should think about it. I know, you're going to tell me to mind my own business. But chaps can still give each other a spot of advice, can't they? I'm not saying women are always easy, but they settle you down, if you see what I mean. You get settled, and you get kids…"

I was utterly speechless. I was staring wide-eyed at the Christmas tree. *There, on the tip of a branch, was my little silvered cage, with its cloth bird inside it.*

I tried to recall whether that was the same branch I had hung it on, but I couldn't be sure. Was I in my right mind? Had I been unhinged by my time inside?

"What's that you're looking at, Mr… er… Herbin?"

I came out of my trance. Everything around me was capsizing, slowly but surely.

I tried to find a viable explanation.

When Dravet came home at some point during the evening he must have gone round in circles in the room before deciding on his fatal course. I imagined he paced up and down, then stopped in front of the tree that had been put up for the little girl he detested, and angrily tore off some of the decorations and threw them in the fireplace or under the furniture.

His wife must have moved the corpse and then come back to tidy up the lounge, and that's when she would have found the decorations—among them, my cage—and then hung them back up on the tree.

"A decorated Christmas tree is a really pretty thing, don't you think?"

"Yes," I muttered. "Very pretty."

Mme Dravet came back in with a smile on her face.

"All done, she went back to sleep in no time. Another drop of cognac, gentlemen?"

"Just a tiny one, because it's Christmas," Ferrie joked.

"I ruined the church service for you."

"Oh, as I was saying to M. Herbin…"

Isn't it odd that she found out what I was called in that way? She shot me a glance that was slightly less sinister than her previous looks.

"… as I was saying to M. Herbin, religion is not my thing. But we've just had a baby boy."

"Congratulations."

The most amazing thing was that the lady of the house seemed really fascinated by the news.

"Just a few ounces short of eight pounds! A real man, don't you think?"

"And what is the young man's name?"

"Jean-Philippe."

"That's lovely."

"You ought to have a drink as well, after what you've just been through," Ferrie advised. He was a spontaneous sort of fellow, and a bit thick as well.

"Of course you must," I chipped in. "For instance, some cherry brandy…"

I took it upon myself to pour her a decent measure.

She downed it in one go.

"Don't you want to call a doctor?"

"No need, it was just a fainting fit. It was so hot…"

"You can say that again!"

She uttered a little scream that made Ferrie and me jump.

"Goodness me!" Mme Dravet sighed.

"What's the matter?"

"I left my handbag in the church!"

Ferrie was too respectful of earthly goods not to share the young woman's dismay.

"Was there a lot inside it?" he asked with urgency.

"Around thirty thousand francs, and my papers..."

"Wow, I see why you're upset. We'll get back down there in no time. There's no reason we shouldn't find it. I'm not saying if you'd left it in a cinema... but in a church, in theory... Am I right?"

He was already on his feet, emptying his glass, doing up his coat.

I stood up too. I couldn't see where Mme Dravet was going with this.

Because I knew she did not have a handbag with her when she left home for the church.

8

The Fourth Visit

"You're not locking the gate?"

"Bah, whatever for?"

He didn't press the point. We went back to Ferrie's Peugeot 403. I opened the door for Mme Dravet. The driver was already at the wheel. I had a few seconds.

"What did you do with the body?" I asked in a single breath.

"Leave me alone, unless you want to get me into trouble. Go back to your flat and I'll come and see you tomorrow."

The driver asked in surprise:

"Are you all right?"

By way of reply she just sat down beside him and pretended not to have heard the question.

The car started up. It was just after one by the clock on the dashboard. I was worn out; I felt as if I was about to pass out, and for good.

Three hundred yards down the road I tapped the driver's shoulder.

"Could you drop me here, please? It's where I live. There's no point my coming with you, right?"

He braked straight away.

"Sure thing. It's not worth your time."

He was not displeased to be left on his own with the woman. It excited him. He'd spent the last few months tending to a pregnant wife and he needed some rest and recreation.

"My best, Madame."

She gave me her hand over the back of the seat.

"Thank you for your kindness."

Ferrie gave my knuckles a vigorous squeeze.

"See you later."

My heart sank as I got out of the car. I stayed standing on the pavement until the two rear lights had quite disappeared.

The whole area had sunk abruptly into the dull and indifferent drowsiness that always comes after a party. Lights were going out in the windows set in the black cliff faces of the blocks of flats. I felt alone, more alone than I had ever been. More alone than with Anna's corpse, more alone than in court or in my cell. I could not make head or tail of Mme Dravet's behaviour. Why had she removed her husband's body? Why the fainting act? Why was she pretending to have left her bag in church when it wasn't true in the least?

My mind kept coming back to the two small red spots on her cuff. At one point I thought she'd killed her husband, and with the help of an accomplice... It was a crazy, outlandish idea, but I was prepared to imagine just about anything, and make myself believe it too.

A few yards away the depressing façade of my block rose up before me like a regret. My whole childhood and my mother were lying in wait for me behind that great peeling wall. I'd wrecked it all and killed the lot of them—my memories, and the people who had made them.

I buttoned up my coat as high as it would go, stuffed my hands in my pockets and, keeping myself as much in the shadows as possible, I went back to the building where the Dravets lived.

I was fed up with the inexplicable and I had to have it out with the young woman. I'd made up my mind to intimidate her if necessary in order to make her talk.

I remembered she'd not locked the main gate, so I went into the bindery yard.

Mysterious reflections gleamed on the large windowpanes. A wild world of imaginary beings pranced about on those tall slats of frosted glass. You had to concentrate on them for quite a while to work out that what you could see were the passing clouds of a foul December night.

I waited for nearly a quarter of an hour and looked over the premises designed for industry. I liked the strong and wholesome smell of paper, and all those reams stacked up like a fortress touched my heart.

Mme Dravet was taking her time. As it was getting colder and colder I took shelter in the cab of one of the lorries. They were parked with their bonnets facing the gate, so I could keep watch on the entrance through the windscreen.

What was she doing with Ferrie? They'd gone to the church; she'd pretended to look for her handbag, and they might even have asked the priest about it. What then? A dummy hunt like that wouldn't take a quarter of an hour! But they'd been gone more than half an hour already!

Fatigue was making me even more numb than I had been in the church. I pulled up my collar, twisted myself round on the bench seat, and put my legs up. I dropped off in no time.

It wasn't proper sleep, but a kind of second state that stood in lieu, with my body in complete repose. I remained alert, only the things around me lost their reality. I was losing my sensitivity to the cold and my interest in the situation. My curiosity was ebbing, and Mme Dravet was turning into the memory of a woman I'd loved and murdered a long time ago.

A car purred to a halt outside the gateway, its engine suddenly switched off, and two doors slammed shut! I woke in a flash with a clear mind made all the sharper by the rest I'd just had.

I wanted to get out of the cab, but it was too late because the gate was already being opened.

I quickly pulled down the sun visor and squeezed myself to the back of the bench seat… I reckoned I would be invisible in the dark.

Mme Dravet came in with Ferrie beside her. The leather-coated gentleman was holding her arm in a familiar manner. She leaned on the gate for a moment.

"Thank you…" she mumbled. "Thank you for everything."

He let go of her arm and stroked her neck as if he had already won her. I was on the point of rushing out of the cab and smashing his face in. It was a bout of acute jealousy like the one I'd suffered one day long ago. A need to destroy what had betrayed me. I saw red. Then suddenly my anger evaporated: she'd just grasped his wrist to make him withdraw his hand.

"So you see, you got a Christmas party in the end," Ferrie was saying.

I allowed myself to make a move inside my hideaway. I released my forearm to look at my watch and it startled me out of my skin. The hands pointed to five ten. So they had been away for more than four hours.

I had a moment of doubt and even put the watch to my ear to check it was still working. Its tranquil tick-tock was a familiar sound. When they'd given it back to me the day before yesterday, the first thing I did was to wind it up and adjust the little second hand. It went back to work obediently.

"You see, Mme Dravet, this has been a special Christmas for me..."

"For me, too."

"Honestly?"

The fool! His voice was all soupy and I'm sure he must have been ogling her like a dead fish.

"You are such an extraordinary woman."

"Nobody has said that to me for such a long time!"

She must have told him about her marital problems as well. Perhaps she also served him up the story of Lucienne's arrival.

"Would you like to come up for one last drink?"

He wasn't expecting this invitation and didn't answer straight away. I was sure he'd been making a play for her energetically throughout the night. She'd put up with it graciously but kept her distance, and then suddenly, when all his hopes were dashed...

"You think I should dare to?"

"Why not? It's Christmas, isn't it?"

They crossed the yard and came within inches of me. Mme Dravet opened the door to the corridor. Then I heard the grating of the lift door. I waited a while before getting out of the lorry.

Instead of going away, I went into the building. I fumbled my way to the stairs and began to go up cautiously, stopping on each step to listen.

I could hear them talking but I could not make out what they were saying. Their voices made a continuous low hum. And all of a sudden came a call:

"Jérôme!" Mme Dravet was shouting. "Jérôme, are you in?"

My blood ran cold. Was the woman mad? Why had she started to call for her husband *when she knew he was dead*?

I put my back to the wall. My heart was racing.

"Jérôme?"

Suddenly, a loud scream. A scream of shock, a scream of madness.

Ferrie's dull voice was stuttering "Madame… Come now, Madame… Madame…"

Then nothing. An abyss of silence that was made even more piercing by the total darkness on the stairwell.

I couldn't move. I was barely breathing. I don't know how long I stayed like that. I should have gone away but some mysterious force kept me there. I wanted to know. Obviously "they" had found the body of Jérôme Dravet. But where had his wife hidden it? And why had she moved it? Why had she delayed the time of discovery? Why? Why? The nightmare was becoming unbearable.

The door on the landing above opened. A tall rectangle of white light plastered itself on the wire surround of the lift shaft. The slim outline of the young woman was silhouetted on the screen of brightness.

A game of shadows. No: a tragedy of shadows. The man in the leather coat was trying to hold her back because she was running away.

"Please stay. The police will be here in a minute. Keep calm, Madame. I'm asking you... I know it's horrible, but you have to... Come, come in... come..."

And he dragged her back into the flat, leaving the front door open.

I stared at the rectangle of light and could hear Mme Dravet sobbing.

I realized I had to get away at all costs. If the police found me on the premises I would be done for.

I started going back down the stone stairs on tiptoe. But just as I got to the bottom steps the sharp pulsing siren of a police van not far off rent the air. I thought I would faint.

The siren stopped. The gate grated on its hinges.

I was caught on the stairs as in a net. My only recourse was to go back up, to put off the final reckoning for a bit.

So I went back up the stairs without bothering to muffle the sound of my shoes. Maybe there would be a way out over the roof? I remembered there was a skylight right over the lift cage.

I got to the landing where there was light. I took a quick look to see whether Mme Dravet or Ferrie were at the doorway. They weren't. Only I saw something else, and it made me doubt my sanity. Through the set of doors that had been left open in the flat, *I clearly saw Jérôme Dravet's corpse set on the sofa in its initial position.*

But I was already past the landing. I began to wonder if I had really seen it, or if I'd been hallucinating.

A narrow wooden stairway went on up to the attic. I climbed it as fast as I could. I could already hear the footsteps of policemen down below. I froze. I couldn't catch my breath. My chest was caught in a terrible, vice-like contraction. There were shouts and whispers two floors down…

My position was untenable. If the police came to look upstairs they would come upon me and then I would never get them to accept that I was there solely as a witness with too much curiosity for his own good. The small staircase went no farther. What should I do?

With infinite caution I ran my hand along the wall as if I were stroking it. My fingers had become a blind man's eyes, they had suddenly acquired a kind of tactile second sight.

I felt the roughness of a door. I found a handle. I turned it, slowly. Slowly. I prayed to God that the door would yield when I pushed it.

The door obeyed. It creaked slightly, but to me that small noise sounded like a gunshot. A few seconds standing stock-still gave me back my courage. I pushed at the door with the utmost wariness. Hope glimmered again. I'd forgotten the stiff downstairs, Mme Dravet's play-acting and the police, and was thinking only about saving my own skin. I knew that attics always had hinged windows on the sloping roof side.

If I found such a thing then it would perhaps be my salvation. But the more I went forward, the darker it got. I was drowning in darkness as if I was sinking into the black earth of a bog.

Once inside the attic room I made to close the door. I did it with even more care than I had opened it.

Once the panel was fully back in place and I'd heard the latch click shut, I reckoned I'd put a tremendous bulwark between myself and the police.

I waited for another minute. I was living in spasms, in disconnected dots.

There was lots of coming and going on the floor below, with people speaking words I couldn't make out and telephones ringing.

"They" should be calling in the medical team and informing the prosecutor's office. Were they going to search the building?

A more insidious fear now gripped me. *I knew Mme Dravet had an accomplice. It had to be so, since while she was away her husband's body had been brought back into the lounge.*

So whoever had done that fearful clean-up job—whether it was a he or a she—could still be in the building. Unless there was another exit I didn't know about. Or unless that person had got away while I was dozing in the cab of the lorry.

Could it have been to help her accomplice that Mme Dravet hadn't bothered to lock the yard gate when she left to look for her supposed handbag?

If the accomplice were in the building, then he or she could be in this very attic! I imagined someone crouching in the dark nearby and ready to slit my throat at the slightest provocation. I thought I could hear faint breathing. I tried to calm myself down, told myself it was my own breathing I could hear, but my fear level went on rising.

Several times I felt like opening the door and going downstairs to meet the police.

What stopped me each time was the thought of the young woman who was caught in a struggle with them. She had asked me to vanish several times over and I'd not done her bidding. I'd persisted in imposing myself and in stalking her. If I made myself known then it would be curtains for her as well as for me.

"Anybody there?" I whispered.

Nobody answered. My voice managed to do what my mind had not. It calmed me down.

If Dravet's wife had an accomplice, then that person would not have been so stupid as to stay on the premises until the police came by.

There was a lot of noise in the staircase now.

"There they go," I thought. "They're searching the building and the bindery."

I waited in a blind funk, expecting the door would burst open and that I would be caught full face in the beam of an electric torch.

But they took their time. Now and again there were pauses in the commotion downstairs. But just when I started hoping again, the noise resumed.

Flashes of optimism, even confidence, alternated with moments when I wanted to weep from fear and misery.

I felt I was too near the stairs. I moved gently towards the back of the room. My elbow bumped into a doorjamb and I could feel I was getting into a more spacious area. I tried to find a skylight but there still wasn't one. I put my hand up to touch the roof but met only air.

As I tried to move farther on, I knocked into something. It must have been a pram (presumably Lucienne's, from when she was a baby) because I could feel the push handle, and when I bumped into it, it moved and made a clatter.

The noise put me back on edge. Had it been heard downstairs?

I had to stay completely still from then on, otherwise I could knock over any one of the discarded objects that people store in attics. With the utmost carefulness I lay down on the floor, on the boards. I found the fringe of an old rug and lay my cheek on it.

Putting your head in the sand is sometimes a good strategy. With my eyes closed and my body completely still I felt invulnerable. If anyone came up and searched the attic with a torchlight, he might even miss me altogether.

Hope returned. Although Dravet's corpse had been handled, suicide remained the most likely explanation and the authorities would probably just go through the motions.

I could make out the sounds of an ambulance bell, of doors being opened and shut, of people calling…

They were still walking and talking on the floor below. Many times I heard the metallic click of a telephone being hung up. Later on there were screams and sobs; at the time, I thought they must have informed Dravet's family and that the wailing came from his relatives.

I looked at my watch. The gleam of its phosphorescent dial made a tiny breach in the dark. In such a total blackout, it stood out like a vision. I couldn't see the watch itself, only the circle of numbers and the two spear-like hands.

Six o'clock… Six twenty… A quarter to seven…

An hour and a half had elapsed since they found the body. So they were not going to search the premises. If the police had suspected anything they would have done a search straight away.

Was I saved?

I hardly dared believe it. I would still have so many hurdles to jump. I would have to leave the attic, get down the stairs, cross the yard.

If there was anyone with Mme Dravet, how could I explain why I was in the building? And if she went out, how would I then open the locked door and the gate?

9

The Switch

I heard the clocks strike seven. Local church bells had long been chiming hours and half hours without my noticing. It's true the building was now completely quiet and that the only noises to reach me came from outside. There was hardly any traffic on this Christmas Day. Heavy delivery vehicles clattered over the cobblestones. A few mopeds were making a racket as they performed incomprehensible circuits around the area.

Should I wait longer? I was in a soggy, lethargic state that deprived me of willpower.

If I waited too long, I would get tangled up in the flood of relatives and friends who would pour in once the news got around. This present inactivity was a window of opportunity that I simply had to make use of.

As I was making ready to stand up I heard someone walking up the wooden staircase leading to the attic with a firm and rapid step. It scared me stiff. Someone was coming and there was no mistake about it. And whoever it was wasn't being shy. He was coming straight at me. The first door opened. The footstep halted for a second. Then it moved closer in more slowly. It was soon a few inches from my face.

The gentle click of a switch and then a stunning surge of light, like when you try to look at the sun for a second. I was blinded by the sudden and utterly unexpected illumination.

In the midst of the glare stood Mme Dravet like some miraculous apparition. My eyes quickly adjusted to the light. She was alone. She had her two hands crossed tightly on her chest and was staring at me with horror, as if I was a profoundly repulsive object.

It's a sure thing that I had just given her the worst scare of her life.

Our eyes crossed in a flash. My attention was captured almost immediately by the décor and I think I screamed. A scream from the gut. The scream of a man thunderstruck by a revelation.

"What are you doing here?" she asked in a grating voice.

Instead of answering, I tried to make sense of it. I wanted to understand the trick. *I wasn't in an attic but in the Dravets' lounge.* There was the sofa, the armchair and the gramophone on the low table. There was the drinks trolley with Ferrie's glass on it and mine, and I suddenly realized it was what I had bumped into in the dark and taken for a pram! There was also the Christmas tree and its tinsel decorations. My silvered cage and its blue and yellow cloth bird were hanging on the tip of a branch like a trinket intended to make fun of me.

The lounge door was of course glazed and I could see the hallway with its coat stand *with no coat hanging on it*.

"Come on, own up, what are you doing here?"

She didn't just sound angry, most of all she sounded in despair.

I put my hands to my head the way ham actors do on stage to express shock and horror.

"I do not understand…"

"You do not understand why you spent the night here?"

"Hang on."

I went over in my mind the path I had taken in the night.

I had climbed one floor. I had gone across the landing in front of the Dravets' flat, and through the open main door I had caught sight of the lounge. A short but complete sight of the room. The corpse was on the sofa…

I had seen the tree, the gramophone, the drinks trolley…

"Hang on."

Something went click inside the exhausted woman. She took two steps forward and sank into the armchair.

"Are you trying to make me believe you haven't got it?" she sighed as she closed her eyes.

I ran out of the lounge to the other end of the hallway. Like a clairvoyant I opened each door as I came to it. All of them opened onto entirely empty rooms with freshly plastered walls that hadn't yet been painted.

Then I went back to her. She had big blue circles under her eyes, and her cheeks looked hollower than before.

"I am dog tired," she murmured. "So tired I wouldn't mind if I died right now."

I sat down on the sofa, facing her. Instinctively, I followed her example in flopping down. We were both completely worn out.

"There are two identical flats on top of each other, right?"

"My father-in-law had the second one built for his second son, who's in the army in Algeria."

I got it. But not really. It was more subtle than that. I grasped that I was on the brink of understanding it all, because I now had all the pieces to put together.

"And you furnished the lounge of this flat exactly like your own place?"

"That wasn't very difficult to do."

"True. You said you were a set designer…"

"You don't need a degree to put a coat of whitewash on a hallway and a lounge, or to buy the same sofa, armchair, gramophone and drinks trolley as the ones you've got already…"

"You murdered him, didn't you?"

"You already know I did."

That was a woman's insight. She'd known my own thoughts before I had.

"You picked me up in the restaurant because you needed a witness."

"Picked…"

"Well, let's say, 'encouraged' me. You played the part perfectly. Every minute seemed to be pure chance, but in reality you were conducting the whole operation with a firm hand!"

"Yes, danger gives you strength."

"So you arranged things to get me in here. You insisted I pour myself a drink."

"*Before leaving this room I had to know what liqueur you would choose.*"

"So you could put the same one in a glass downstairs?"

She nodded. Underneath it all, was she really bothered by my being there? Wasn't she secretly pleased to have someone to confide in? Wasn't her strange secret too heavy to bear alone?

"And you put on a record because of the bang?"

"Obviously."

I grinned.

"Wagner! Right man for the job…"

Time passed and she didn't say a word. She wanted to confess, but only in the way clumsy penitents confess, by responding to questions.

I had a hundred questions, a thousand questions, too many questions to ask. I didn't know which to choose.

The simplest way to get to the bottom of Dravet's murder was by following chronological order.

"When you left this room you went down one floor with Lucienne?"

Hearing her daughter's name brought tears to her eyes. I saw them form into drops on the tips of her long lashes and pause there for a minute before breaking free and flowing down her beautiful, tortured face.

"You put her to bed quickly?"

She nodded in a way that could have been taken for a yes but I think that the truth is she wanted to shake away more tears that were forming under her eyelashes.

"Then you went into the lounge—the real one—to kill your husband, for that's where he was. But, to start with, I don't understand…"

"At noon I'd given him three delayed-action phenobarbital capsules inside chocolates. They contain several different sleep-inducing substances that are released in sequence. With the right dose, you can put someone to sleep for hours and hours…"

93

A faint smile puckered her lips for an instant.

"The proof of it being…"

"So, he was asleep?"

"Yes."

She knew full well what I was thinking. If things went badly for her, no jury would allow for mitigating circumstances. She had killed a sleeping man in cold blood with lengthy, cunning and patient premeditation.

"I scare you, don't I? You think I am a monster."

I shrugged.

"It's not for a man like me to judge you."

She put out her hand very gently, the way she had in the cinema. For a split second I thought it was starting all over again.

I took her hand and squeezed it. All I asked from the heavens was a few minutes' respite. I was expecting a ring of the doorbell or the tinny sound of the telephone.

"Nobody was concerned about him being away yesterday afternoon?"

"One person: his mistress. In the morning the bindery was open and working. She went to see him quite shamelessly in his office and my husband's secretary told me they had had a row about Christmas Eve. In the late afternoon she telephoned the flat, without saying who she was. She wanted to speak to Jérôme. I said he'd gone out."

"I hope the police know about the argument?"

"They must."

"It supports the suicide story. By the way, how did the cops react?"

She thought for a moment.

"I don't know."

"Well, what attitude did they take?"

"They're like doctors, they don't say anything. They took photographs and made measurements. They put the gun into a plastic bag."

"And then?"

"They sealed the lounge door!"

I didn't like the sound of that. I imagined that when the police have a clear case of suicide on their hands they don't take so many precautions.

But that was just the opinion of a non-professional. If the police had really suspected something, they would have searched the whole building.

"OK. You killed him… You had gloves on, I suppose?"

"Yes. But he pulled the trigger. I just held his hand, you see."

Like you hold the hand of an illiterate to make him sign his name. She had made Dravet sign his own death.

"Two drops of blood spattered your cuff."

"I noticed you were worried about those stains. They bothered you before we found the body. I almost ditched you when we came out of the café."

They were harsh words, but she softened them by little squeezes of her hand.

"What did you do with the gloves?"

"I dropped them down a sewer grating during our walk in the moonlight; didn't you notice?"

"No," I confessed, rather pathetically.

I wanted to know every detail. There was something spectacular about the affair that fascinated me.

"So you shot him, and then?"

"I poured a drop of cognac in one glass and a drop of cherry brandy in the other… I put both glasses on the shelf of the drinks trolley."

"So that's why when we were about to go out a bit later you took the glass I'd put on the mantelpiece and placed it on the trolley *the way it was downstairs*?"

"Did you notice?"

"Well, you can see…"

"We chatted. We went out."

"And when we came back you stopped the lift on the first floor instead of the second. So I wouldn't notice the difference in the time it took, you kissed me…"

"Do you think that's the only reason?"

"Tell me about that goods lift."

"It goes up two floors, in fact. The factory has been designed quite rationally. Gluing is done on the first floor and packaging on the second. When he designed the premises my husband wanted the lift to serve both the factory and the flat and that's why it has doors on both sides."

"So?"

"This evening I unscrewed and took out the switch for the second floor as an ultimate precaution, to make sure my 'visitor-witness' wouldn't even imagine there was a second floor."

"But you took me up to the second floor on my first visit! How did you manage that?"

"I had a child-sized thimble which I could insert in lieu of the second-floor switch. The tip of the thimble just fitted inside the switch-hole on the control panel. Logically I would need to go to the second floor once only, since the tragedy would be discovered on the second visit..."

"My congratulations. You are very cunning."

I wondered, as I looked at her, how Machiavellian scheming and meticulous planning of such a high order could have sprung forth from that woman's soul.

"And I switched the bulbs in the hall and the lift with broken ones."

Now she needed to go the whole hog. She wanted to impress me.

"When you came the first time carrying Lucienne in your arms I stopped the lift a little short of the floor. I did the same on your third visit when you came with that man from the church... Do you know why?"

"No."

"Because our flat on the first floor is not exactly level with the first floor of the factory. Since the lift was installed primarily for the factory, there's a step up when you get out of it on the flat side. But on the second floor the flat and the factory floors are on the same level. So I had to create an artificial step by halting the lift a bit before its normal level."

"Bravo. That can't have been easy in complete darkness."

"I spent nights practising it when I was here on my own. It's turned into a kind of reflex. I'm now able to stop the lift within an inch of the same place."

'When I was here on my own…' That set me thinking what this woman's life must have been like, in these industrial premises, with her rejected daughter.

She had indeed had all the time she needed to design a murder. To gear herself up for it, and also to set the wheels in motion. To take it on like a job…

"How come the door of the second-floor flat wasn't locked? I only had to turn the handle to get in."

"For safety's sake."

"Meaning?"

"I only pretended to use a key on each occasion. In fact I used the key to the downstairs flat to fiddle around with the lock up here, so as to create the illusion. I was afraid that in the police inquiry they would start by asking for my set of keys and that the upstairs key would attract their attention. Because my husband didn't have a key to this flat, and I was afraid they would compare our two sets."

I let go of Mme Dravet's hand.

"And to think I nearly wrecked such a perfect and meticulous plan."

She nodded.

"Yes. I stumbled on the only man in the area I couldn't use as a witness. When you confessed who… who you were, I could almost have killed myself… I was back to square one."

"So did you go back to square one?"

"Only it was getting very risky, because the body was cooling down. That's why I did what I had to, to stay out with Ferrie for several hours. It was the only possible solution: to add lots of time, so they wouldn't be able to establish the time of death with any precision… I dragged Ferrie off to a noisy place where we made an exhibition of ourselves. We put on paper hats, threw streamers, drank champagne. He said it was the best Christmas party he'd ever been to."

She drooped from weariness.

"Do you think they'll do an autopsy?"

"If they're in any doubt, they surely will."

"Allegedly, the capsules don't leave any traces. There's just the issue of the trajectory… But I think I got that right…"

Her voice was calm and her face looked like that of any other sensible young woman. They made it hard to believe what she'd done and especially the circumstances in which she had done it.

"As for the timing," she went on, "who could possibly query it if there's no autopsy! And even if there is one! Ferrie testified that the lounge was empty when we went out. He testified that he never let me out of his sight. He testified that he found my husband's body *at the same time as I did.*"

She stood up and came right up to my knees. She put her hand under my chin.

"Now, you are the only danger I face. What does it feel like to hold somebody's life in your hands?"

She was asking *me*?

For it was she who had killed a man.

And I had killed a woman.

10

The Cloth Bird

"So why did you kill him?"

She shook her head.

"I would rather not explain. Because of my daughter. Jérôme was so odious to that child…"

I blurted out:

"You're not going to tell me you wanted to put that man's corpse in her Christmas stocking?"

She uttered a cruel laugh.

"No, I'm not going to say that. But you know, Albert, you're not too far from the truth!"

She remembered my first name! That's all it takes to win over a man. Up to that point I'd felt vaguely humiliated by being made a mug of by that woman. But wasn't it really fate herself that had thrust the role upon me? Wasn't it only a convoluted set of circumstances even more delicately engineered than the murder of Dravet that had brought me to the table next to hers in the restaurant?

The previous day I'd woken up in prison a thousand kilometres away and yet an unlikely web of apparently minor, random events had led me inexorably to that encounter.

"Your act in the church was sheer genius."

"I got the idea from you. When you telephoned I was in

Lucienne's room. I was watching her sleep and wondering how some mothers manage to do away with themselves along with their children. I was trying to find the recipe for such an awful thing. When I saw you standing in the crowd when I was being carried out of the church, I almost screamed in despair."

"Tell me, did you mention me in your statement?"

"Ferrie talked about you. But as you weren't present when the body was found, the police didn't seem to give it much weight..."

"Will they be back?"

"Probably. I got lumbered with relatives and with prosecutors who hadn't woken up properly. They'd all had too much to drink and too little sleep. It was a nightmare... I think the coast will be clear until noon. They all need to get some sleep, don't they?"

"You came up here to clear the room out?"

"Yes. I don't have a lot of time to do it..."

She was waiting for my verdict. Mme Dravet had spoken the plain truth when she said I had her life in my hands.

I cast my now enlightened eyes around the room. It wasn't a real room now, just a stage set. A set reproducing every detail of the lounge where the tragedy had occurred.

"What are you going to do with the furniture?"

"The armchair makes a pair with the one downstairs. It's the one I'm supposed to have taken out to make room for the Christmas tree. I just have to get it down into one of the other rooms, the dining room for instance, the police hardly went into it... And I was going to put the bottles away in the kitchen.

The gramophone and the drinks trolley are to be smashed up and burned in the huge central heating furnace, along with the tree. Only the sofa can stay here. I sewed a cover for it in a different colour that alters its appearance quite radically…"

"OK, good," I decided. "Let's get on with it!"

I was well aware she was hoping I would keep my mouth shut, but she hadn't been expecting me to offer any help. My decision to do so gave her quite a fright.

I looked at the time. I felt very much in control of myself. The murder was a masterpiece of its kind and I wanted to make my own contribution to it.

It was almost eight. Would we be granted an hour's respite?

With Mme Dravet's help I carried the armchair, the drinks trolley, the gramophone and the low table it stood on into the goods lift.

We put the armchair in the first-floor dining room as she had planned. Then we went down to the basement. Dismantling the trolley, the gramophone and the low table was child's play. Especially because, given the size of the boiler's firebox, we didn't need to break them up into small pieces.

When it had all been consumed by the flames and the metal insides of the gramophone had been reduced to a small tangle of blackened steel, I replenished the boiler with coal.

We were as red as scalded tomatoes when we got back up to the second floor. We still had to strip the tree of the various trinkets that were hung on it and then saw it up so we could burn it. We got to work without talking to each other. We kept at it with feverish, dizzying haste. The more the room ceased to look like the one on the floor below, the more we became aware of the thinness of the ice on which we were skating. A policeman could turn up any moment and find me in the Dravets' flat, or have a mind to search the house from the bottom… to the top!

She uttered a little cry when she came upon my cage with the cloth bird. She looked at it suspiciously.

I then told her where the decoration came from and she started to weep. She sat on the sofa and sobbed convulsively, clutching the flimsy gewgaw to her breast.

"Why are you crying like that?" I asked her when she began to calm down.

"Because of you, Albert. I'm thinking of you buying that in a shop all on your own, without knowing what you would do with it."

She was capable of planning her husband's death for weeks on end, she was capable of firing a bullet at point blank range into a sleeping man's brain, and yet she was weeping over a trinket that symbolized my loneliness.

"I don't want you to throw it away."

"But how can you put it on the other tree if the room is sealed?"

"I'll hang it over Lucienne's bed. I don't know if a woman like me has any right to believe in lucky charms, but it seems to me that's what this little bird is. I believe it will protect my daughter…"

And then she went downstairs straight away with the glitter-dusted cardboard cage. I still had to split off the branches from the tree. I went down to the basement to do that. When

I opened the firebox to throw in the wood, thick black smoke poured out. And each time I opened the cast-iron door, a suffocating cloud smelling of tree resin swirled out from the grate.

The glass baubles we'd put in a little box looked like very precious eggs. I stuffed them into the boiler in one go and they burst with the sound of crushed biscuit.

I swept up the green pine needles on the basement floor. After that I went upstairs. As I reached the main door on the landing of the first floor, I heard Mme Dravet's voice. I thought she was on the telephone, and went inside with measured step. That's when I heard a man's voice, too. I wanted to beat a retreat, only I could hear someone coming up the stairs behind me. I was trapped. In front of me was a visitor in full flow in the dining room. Behind me, new arrivals.

Straight opposite was the "lounge of tragedy" with its door sealed with pieces of wax the colour of dried blood.

I played my last card. I tiptoed down the corridor to the nearest door, the child's bedroom.

I don't think it's possible to enter a room more quickly or more surreptitiously than I did that time.

The girl's room was in grey half-light. My silvered cage was hanging from the bedpost. Lucienne's breathing was light and regular. This little room was touchingly stuffy.

A few inches away, footsteps made the floorboards creak. Voices hummed.

Someone would surely come in eventually. I cast around for a hiding place but didn't find one. There was nothing in the room apart from the bed, a small painted wardrobe and a pile of toys.

Was it my presence that disturbed the child's sleep, or the comings and goings in the next room? Suddenly she let out a cry. It sounded like a high-pitched lament of a vaguely animal kind.

I'd been through too many strong feelings that night. That cry cut into me like a surgeon's knife into anaesthetized flesh.

"It's my daughter waking up," Mme Dravet explained to whoever was there. She was on her way. With someone.

I threw myself behind the bed. I must have stuck out on both sides. Once again I was putting my head in the sand.

The door opened. The mother came in. There was a man with her, but he stayed at the door, and that's what saved me. As she came up to the bed Mme Dravet saw me, and I saw just how much self-control she possessed.

She didn't stray from her path, picked up the child, and went out with her in such a way as to give me maximum cover from the door.

I was left on my own in the room with its grinning plywood Donald Ducks. On my own except for the blue and yellow cloth bird swinging away on its perch.

11

Lost Property

I'd almost lost track of time when they left, as I had done in the cab of the lorry during the night. In any case I wasn't entirely sure they had all gone. I only learned for certain when Mme Dravet started chanting outside the door what she had to tell me in a way that didn't arouse the child's attention.

> There we are, they've all gone, tra la
> I'm taking her into the kitchen now
> Go into the lounge will you please
> Then I can get her back to bed, tra la

That's how I was able to leave the bedroom without being seen by Lucienne. Her mother was with me a minute later.

She looked very downcast.

"You were as scared as I was, weren't you?" I stuttered as I put my arms around her.

She cuddled up to me in complete surrender. She was done in.

"They rang the bell. I thought you had heard from the basement and had hidden down there."

"I didn't hear a thing. I was a split second away from walking right into them. What were they after?"

"To check up on things, they said. They took off the seals, and then resealed the lounge. I don't know what they did in there; while some of them were at it, others were questioning me in the dining room."

"About me?"

"Actually, yes, they did refer to you. But most of it was about my husband's girlfriend."

"What did they want to know?"

"Not much about you: how did I know you; do you remember coming out of the church; do you remember the people who came up to you. I said I knew absolutely nothing about you, that it's quite possible you noticed me but there was nothing mutual about it."

"That was the right thing to say. What about the girlfriend?"

"Well, that was an inquisition. They wanted to know if I was aware of the affair, and so forth, you know what I mean."

"I hope I do."

I sneaked a kiss in her hair.

"They didn't go upstairs?"

"No."

"Thank God. Let's go up and finish it off. Are you sure none of them has stayed behind in the building?"

"I saw them all as far as the main gate and locked it securely behind them."

"Did they question Lucienne as well?"

"Not at all. One of the detectives even asked me if he could give her a chocolate wrapped in gold paper that he had in his pocket."

"All good. Let's go up."

I'd started to feel it was my murder too. I'd accepted it and made it my own.

All we still had to do was to put the dust cover on the second-floor sofa and sweep up with care. I took on the lowly task of sweeping while Mme Dravet added a supremely elegant twist to the scene change by rehanging the heavy curtains inside out. She'd put in a white lining, so with the lining facing in they completed the room's empty, blank look.

"Where's the dust cover for the sofa?"

"Under the seat cushions!"

She had really left nothing to chance. I swiftly pulled out the cushions and yes, there was the cover, neatly folded lengthwise. But as I picked it up something fell out: a cheap, flat plastic slipcase with a transparent panel, such as you put an ID card in. What was in it was a registration document in the name of a certain Paul Ferrie, residing in Paris, for a Citroën delivery van.

I looked at the document with a worried eye.

"What is it?" Mme Dravet asked.

I handed her the mock-crocodile slipcase.

"The fool lost his registration card by lolling on the sofa on his first visit here."

She didn't move, and stood there looking hard at the document as if it represented a tricky problem for her to solve.

"You look concerned," I mumbled uneasily.

"I'm thinking."

"About what?"

"I'm thinking that Ferrie is going to notice he's lost a thing that he needs and he's going to wonder where he might have dropped it."

"And so?"

She didn't answer straight away. She was a thorough woman who thought things all the way through.

"So nothing. He'll certainly come back here to look for it."

"Probably, but that's not a risk. Now take a look…"

I picked up the dust cover and draped it over the sofa. I tucked the edges under the seat cushions and smoothed it over the back. I pushed it to the back of the room with my knee. It now looked like a flat undergoing redecoration. Absolutely nothing like the lounge one level down, apart from the floor plan and the colour of the walls.

Mme Dravet retreated to the hall.

"Your eyes are fresher than mine, so tell me, do you think Ferrie would have the slightest suspicion if he came up here?"

I closed my eyes for a moment to clear my vision, and then opened them on the new décor.

"No, he could not possibly. The copycat effect doesn't come from the shape of the lounge, but from the tree, the trolley, the gramophone. Mme Dravet, I sincerely believe you have pulled off the perfect crime. Even if the police discover it wasn't suicide but murder, they will never be able to pin it on you."

She still had the plastic slipcase in her hand and was fanning her cheek with it.

"What are we going to do with this?"

"Give it to me, I'll go and lose it in the church."

"You think that's safe?"

"Of course it is. It's the kind of thing people always hand in to the police, whether they're honest folk or not. Someone will be eager to get a reputation for being a good citizen by turning it in."

I stuffed it into my pocket. I now had two difficult tasks ahead of me. One, to take my leave of Mme Dravet; two, to get out of the building without being seen by a policeman who could be out there keeping watch.

"Are there any other ways out of the bindery?"

"There's a door from the office to the street."

"Do you think the police know about that exit?"

She shrugged her shoulders.

"If the police have the building under surveillance, they are bound to be aware of all the access points."

I was at a loss. If they were on the lookout, then I would wreck the whole plan by going out.

On the other hand, I couldn't stay at J. Dravet & Co. forever more!

After a moment's thought, my companion mumbled:

"But there is a third exit."

"Where is it?"

"It's a kind of chute that's used for rolls of paper. Yes, that's the solution. The police can't know about it. It comes out in a wide cul-de-sac where lorries can back in so as not to obstruct traffic. Come on…"

I took a last look around. Some people, when they wake up, are sorry to leave their dreams behind, even if they've been nightmares. I was in the same boat.

We went down the staircase this time. On the first-floor landing I paused for a moment, as if to say farewell to the little girl asleep in the flat.

We went into the bindery, a bright, well-lit place littered with scraps of paper. It had a wholesome smell of labour and, despite my weariness, I felt a great will to work surge up in me. I would look for a job first thing in the morning.

"You see, here it is."

The chute door consisted of twin cast-iron shutters, with a huge bolt to close them by. It was at the top of a cement slipway. I pushed one of the panels. It was quite wide enough for me to get through.

"Well, there we are," she murmured as she took my arm. "This is the parting of our ways. In the circumstances, I don't think it would be quite appropriate to say 'thank you'."

"There's no right word. What happened was in another place with other rules."

We looked at each other with sweet sadness that hurt but also comforted us both.

"I don't know if we'll ever see each other again," she said, closing her eyelids.

"I hope we do, with all my soul, as you know."

"I think we have to let some time go by…"

"So do I. You know where I live and I know where you live. There's no reason we shouldn't meet again one day."

I left the factory without another word, and pulled the trapdoor shut behind me. It made a very fulsome and vibrant sound as it closed. I heard the screech of the great bolt, and the vast sadness that came upon me at that point signalled the fact that I was once again entirely on my own.

12

You Never Can Tell

There was nobody at the cul-de-sac exit. Nor was there anyone on the street. Our fears had been unnecessary and our precautions uncalled for. The police had swallowed the suicide story.

This Christmas morning was sinister—overcast, with a cold breeze sure to bring snow. The area felt dead and the few passers-by who hurried along close to the walls to keep out of the wind had faces even more grey than the sky.

I was absolutely shattered. The only thing in my mind was to have a wash and climb into a warm bed. My murky labours in the Dravets' basement had crumpled and soiled my clothes. I could see my reflection in shop windows and it wasn't an encouraging sight. I looked as limp and washed-out as the flags you see flying on public monuments.

I looked over my shoulder several times, but there was nobody on my tail. I remember having a dizzy spell from the view down a completely empty avenue with trees pruned right down to the trunk, looking like the stumps of amputated limbs.

This time my building depressed me less than before. It had put on the cheerful face it used to have in the old days, the way it looked when I came home from school.

I looked for the pot of geraniums on the windowsill of our flat. The pot was still there, but not the geraniums. The plant must have died after Ma, for want of care.

I strode up the wooden staircase. I wasn't taken aback any more by the smell of bleach and dusty carpets. I opened the door to "home", the old dwelling that was chock full of my memories. There was one for each of my moods.

I dashed to the sink to wash, because that was the most urgent thing, but the sight of the brass tap all green with tarnish reminded me that there was no water in it any more. A hotel would be a better bet. Only it would look suspicious if I turned up at such an hour without any luggage. So I put a clean shirt and suit in a suitcase. Ma had mothballed my clothes in plastic slipcovers to await my return. They were obviously out of fashion now, but I was glad to get them back.

Off I went again, carrying the scuffed old suitcase with a clasp that kept on springing open. I walked fast because I was in a hurry to find a resting place. I was going to treat myself to a room with a bath. I would have a very hot bath and then lie naked in bed and sink into blessed oblivion.

I was crossing the square in front of the church when I remembered I had Ferrie's registration card in my pocket. I'd almost forgotten about it. I took it out discreetly and dropped it on the pavement next to a tree. As I went on my way a voice hailed me:

"Hey there, sir! You've dropped something!"

I turned around slowly, feeling merely irritated by this nuisance. It reminded me of an American movie I had seen in prison, the story of a guy who never managed to get rid of something he wanted to lose. It was full of unbelievable set-ups. Every time he left the object somewhere, some outside event obliged him to take it back. In the end he found himself at home unwrapping the package in a temper, only to discover it wasn't the same thing he'd started off with.

The man who'd hailed me was fairly stout. He was wearing a black loden, a grey hat with an upturned brim, and had an empty cigarette holder stuck between his teeth.

I pretended to be surprised.

"You mean me?"

He came right up to me, apparently delighted to be doing a good deed for his fellow man. People say most humans are evil, but it's not true, the world is full of altruists.

He picked up the slipcase himself.

"I saw it fall out of your pocket. It is yours, isn't it?"

"Oh, yes! Thank you so much…"

I smiled as I put out my hand to take the registration card. But instead of giving it to me, the man glanced at it and then slipped it into his own pocket.

I didn't understand why he was behaving so illogically.

He turned over the lapel of his loden. Underneath was a brightly burnished badge showing he was a member of the Paris police.

"Follow me, Herbin."

I had to react, to say something.

"I don't understand."

"No, but we can explain."

He put up his arm and a car pulled up. I didn't see where it came from. Presumably it had been tailing the policeman at a distance. It was an old Frégate with dented wings. The driver was a man in a parka with a narrow-rimmed green felt hat.

"Get in!" the policeman in the loden commanded.

"But on what grounds? What right do you have…?"

He didn't waste any time explaining. He just gave me a hefty thump in the back that toppled me forward into the vehicle. I tripped over my poor suitcase and ended up on my knees on the torn rubber floor mat.

The loden man seated himself beside me on the rear bench with a grunt of relief. The car moved off.

Nobody said anything. I tried to sort it out in my mind. Had I been followed all the way from the Dravets'? I was sure I hadn't been. Absolutely certain. On the other hand, I did now recall seeing this big black car parked opposite the building where I lived.

Yes, they'd put a watch on my place. Luckily!

I had to understand why the police had taken these measures if I was going to get myself out of the hole I was in. It wasn't complicated. The detectives wanted to get hold of "the other witness", that's to say, me. And that was child's play for them, since I'd stupidly given my name to Ferrie when we'd been introduced in the switch lounge. In addition, he knew which street I lived in. Hadn't I had him pull up almost in front of my building?

Over the last few hours the police had made some inquiries. They'd found out who I was and where I came from.

I told myself to keep calm. I wanted to remain hopeful.

They were going to ask me where I'd spent the night and especially where I'd found Ferrie's registration card.

The Frégate came to a halt at the foot of a set of grey steps. Over the door there was a flag just like the one I had compared myself to a few moments before.

"Keep moving!"

An office corridor with policemen standing round paying no attention to me and talking among themselves about their Christmas parties and their kids.

An office, wooden benches, wall posters, green shades, a smell of ink, mouldy paper, sweat...

"Sit down!"

Apart from the thump they'd given me at the start, they weren't treating me roughly. I hung on, believing it would work out. When danger is right in front of you, it's less scary.

Now, let's see, I spent the night in local bars. Most of them were packed, which would account for nobody noticing me. As for that damned registration document... Well, I found the card in Ferrie's car. I thought the slipcase had come out of my own pocket and didn't notice my mistake until much later.

I just had to stick to my guns, come what may.

They had nothing on me.

I said it to myself over and over again as if trying to make myself believe it. If I were truly convinced of it, I would manage to get myself out of this sticky situation.

I thought about Mme Dravet. I was sorry not to have asked her what her first name was, it would have been more convenient to think about her that way. I'd never met anyone so surprising. She had ferocious willpower and an astounding presence of mind, and yet I knew she was a weak and lost soul. We were birds of a feather, she and I.

116

The detective in the loden was talking about his children's toys to a colleague who was re-rolling a broken cigarette in a second piece of gummed paper. For them, it was still Christmas Day, despite having to deal with a new case. At home they had a tree, sweets, lights, joy, children shouting, and a sliver of all that came with them into this dismal place.

"Herbin!"

The other detective, the one in the parka, motioned me into an office.

A man of about fifty with a comical bald patch that made his scalp look like it was made of cardboard was sitting behind an official desk piled high with paperwork. He had a big nose that was quite circular and a tuft of black moustache beneath it.

He pointed me to a chair upholstered in leather that bore scratch marks made by fingernails.

"Albert Herbin?"

He had his eyes on a set of pencilled notes and didn't raise them to speak to me.

"Yes, sir."

"Released the day before yesterday at dawn from Baumettes prison in Marseilles?"

I corrected him.

"No, yesterday morning."

Then I worked it out. My grasp of time had got a bit hazy because of the two nights in a row without sleep.

"Pardon me, you're right. It was the day before yesterday."

"How did you come up from Marseilles?"

"On the night train."

"And since then?"

I shrugged. He was looking straight at me now. He had a peaceable look and calm eyes, but there was a dangerous glint at the back of them.

"I went back to my mother's home. Then I enjoyed being out and free."

"In what way?"

"The only way there is: I wandered round the streets, I dropped into bars, I looked at the new cars that had come out since I'd been inside. The world changes in six years, you know. Catching up is hard to do."

"You went to Midnight Mass?"

We were getting to the point. He didn't really want to beat about the bush.

"Indeed I did."

"During the service, a lady was taken ill?"

"Yes... Mme..."

I pretended to be trying to remember the name.

"Drevet, or Dravet, right?"

"Yes."

He raised his voice when he gave me this assent. It was a provocative assent.

"Did you tell the people who took her out of the church that you were acquainted with her?"

"Absolutely not! I said I knew where she lived, that's not the same thing!"

"And how did you come to know her address?"

"That's easy. On a walk round the area, I saw her coming out of her place with her little girl. I haven't seen a woman or a child in six years. These ones were pretty so I noticed them. And in church I recognized them, that's all."

"Didn't you in fact follow them to the church?"

"No."

"It appears that while in prison you were not an attender of religious services."

"So what?"

"But as soon as you're out the first thing you do is go to church."

"Midnight Mass is a spectacle for lots of people! And that particular church is 'my' church! I went in search of my childhood…"

He batted his eyelids. He understood completely, and I could feel he was a bit taken aback because of the Christmas atmosphere that alters things and people a bit.

"All right. And then?"

"I took the lady and her daughter back to their home along with another obliging gentleman who happened to be there."

"Next?"

I could hear a slight noise behind me and I turned round to look. The man with the parka was taking down notes on a large sheet of paper.

"We escorted Mme… er…"

"Dravet!"

He wasn't taken in and guessed I was only pretending not to remember…

"… Mme Dravet up to her flat. We had a drink in her lounge while she put her child to bed. When she came back in she realized she'd left her handbag at the church. So we went out again and I asked the driver to drop me off near my place."

He picked up the plastic slipcover and waved it at me.

"And this?"

"Ah yes. When we left Mme Dravet's I dropped my key in the car. I picked it up and scooped that up along with it. I thought it was mine and…"

Wrong track! I could see a gleam in my interrogator's eyes that brought me to a halt.

He didn't believe me! He didn't just think I was lying, *he had proof!*

"So you claim that you picked up this registration card in Mr Ferrie's car?"

"Yes."

"You're quite sure?"

"Yes."

All of a sudden he relaxed, slackening the tension in his whole substantial body. He leaned back in his chair and stared at me with an insulting grin.

"You are lying, Herbin."

"No, I'm not."

He brought his fat hand down hard on the leather-topped desk.

"Yes, you are. I'll prove it to you…"

He turned to the detective in the parka and ordered:

"Bring in Ferrie."

The leather-coated man came into the office. He was still wearing his coat and came forward with a deferential bow. He smiled kindly as he saw me.

"Oh! Hello, Herbin. Quite a hoo-ha, isn't it!"

I didn't move, and he looked at the detective with an astonished air. The bald man was waving his registration card.

"Ah! You've got it back!" Ferrie exclaimed. "You see, I was right!…"

"One moment, Mr Ferrie," the detective interrupted. "Would you please tell Mr Herbin where your registration card was?"

Ferrie looked embarrassed.

"Ah, well, it's not very clever, but when we were at Mme Dravet's that evening, I secretly put the card under the sofa cushion. I… Well, boys will be boys, Herbin! You know how it is. I thought it would give me an excuse to come back to look for it later on that night. A little lady all on her own at home might be a golden opportunity… for a temporarily unattached man… As you were there too, I didn't dare chat her up openly. If I'd known that she was going to ask to go out again and then stay with me, obviously I… And especially if I'd had any inkling that when we got back…"

I braced myself to smile at him. But I was turning to ice.

"When we found her husband's body, the bloody card went plain out of my mind. But when I got home and saw my van in the garage, it came back to me. So I went to these gentlemen to explain…"

The chief inspector clicked his fingers.

"Thank you, Mr Ferrie. You may go now."

Ferrie was taken aback and just stood there with his mouth open for a moment. Then he nodded his head and backed out of the room.

The chief inspector put his hands together on the edge of the desk.

"There you are, Herbin."

"I am innocent!" I shouted at the top of my voice.

"You're not up to much. You didn't even act surprised when Ferrie mentioned the husband's corpse."

I must have had a funny look because he burst out laughing. I couldn't take any more. That laugh completely annihilated me.

"Got that down, Bache?"

"Yes, sir."

The bald man leaned forward. His bulging paunch squashed up against his old leather writing set. His face was inches from mine. I felt sick, his breath smelt of milky coffee.

"Listen carefully, Herbin. When the three of you left the Dravets', the registration card was under the sofa cushion. When Ferrie and Mme Dravet came back, they found a stiff, M. Dravet, and didn't touch anything. After Ferrie's statement this morning, my men went back to search the sofa, and the registration document wasn't there. I therefore conclude that you entered Mme Dravet's flat while she was out. You knew the only person there was the baby, providing a perfect opportunity for a man with no money who's just out of jail. Only Jérôme Dravet came back in while you were looking over the place. He pulled his gun on you. You disarmed him and shot him point blank. In the course of the struggle the sofa cushions got thrown about and when you were putting them back in place you came across Ferrie's registration card. Why did you take it? A stupid reflex action. Stupid, and also dangerous, since it has allowed us to catch you out."

He talked and talked, quite sure of himself and of being right.

I'd stopped listening to him. My mind had wandered back into the strange labyrinth. *There now was only one lounge at the Dravets'! I had destroyed the traces of the switch by my own hand.*

I could try telling them the truth, but I didn't care to. How could I get them to believe such a truth? Nightmares are personal things that become absurd when you try to tell them to other people. You can experience them, that's all you can do…

The blue and yellow bird swinging over the bed of the little girl came to my mind. All I'd done with my time out of prison was to buy a silver-spangled cage. What a symbol! I was going to go back into a cage. Unless Mme Dravet, on learning of my arrest…

"Tell me, inspector…"

I must have cut him off in full flight. He went red in the face and looked aghast when he suddenly realized that I hadn't even been listening to him.

"What?"

"What is Mme Dravet's first name, please?"

He looked at me, then at his sidekick, then at a piece of paper on his desk.

"Marthe," he bellowed spitefully.

"Thank you."

There was nothing more for me to say.

Marthe would have to decide what to do.

———

♥ Did you know?

One of France's most prolific and popular post-war writers, Frédéric Dard wrote no fewer than 284 thrillers over his career, selling more than 200 million copies in France alone. The actual number of titles he authored is under dispute, as he wrote under at least 17 different aliases (including the wonderful Cornel Milk and l'Ange Noir).

Dard's most famous creation was San-Antonio, a James Bond-esque French secret agent, whose enormously popular adventures appeared under the San-Antonio pen name between 1949 and 2001. The thriller in your hands, however, is one of Dard's "novels of the night" – a run of stand-alone, dark psychological thrillers written by Dard in his prime, and considered by many to be his best work.

Dard was greatly influenced by the great Georges Simenon. A mutual respect developed between the two, and eventually Simenon agreed to let Dard adapt one of his books for the stage in 1953. Dard was also a famous inventor of words – in fact, he dreamt up so many words and phrases in his lifetime that a 'Dicodard' was recently published to list them all.

Dard's life was punctuated by drama; he attempted to hang himself when his first marriage ended, and in 1983 his daughter was kidnapped and held prisoner for 55 hours before being ransomed back to him for 2 million francs. He admitted afterwards that the experience traumatised him for ever, but he nonetheless used it as material for one of his later novels. This was typical of Dard, who drew heavily on his own life to fuel his extraordinary output of three to five novels every year. In fact, when contemplating his own death, Dard said his one regret was that he would not be able to write about it.

So, where do you go from here?

If you feel like another novel of the night, take a look at Dard's paranoid prison-escape classic, *The Wicked Go to Hell*.

Or if you're after something that packs more of a punch, pick up a copy of Martin Holmén's ultra-gritty Scandi-noir debut, *Clinch*.

AVAILABLE AND COMING SOON
FROM PUSHKIN VERTIGO

Jonathan Ames

You Were Never Really Here

Augusto De Angelis

The Murdered Banker
The Mystery of the Three Orchids
The Hotel of the Three Roses

María Angélica Bosco

Death Going Down

Piero Chiara

The Disappearance of Signora Giulia

Frédéric Dard

Bird in a Cage
Crush
The Wicked Go to Hell

Martin Holmén

Clinch

Alexander Lernet-Holenia

I Was Jack Mortimer

Boileau-Narcejac

Vertigo
She Who Was No More

Leo Perutz

Master of the Day of Judgment
Little Apple
St Peter's Snow

Soji Shimada

The Tokyo Zodiac Murders

Seishi Yokomizo

The Inugami Clan